Crazy Little Thing Called Dead

A Bree MacGowan Mystery

by Kate George

Find more from Kate George at
http://kategeorge.com/

First Print Edition: October 2012

Dedication

For the BBs,
Toni, Carol-Ann, Kim, Karen, Jude, Susan, Sara, Lora,
Doreen, Emily and Tanya.
You ladies are the best!

Acknowledgements

Thanks to Denise Perkins of Planet Hair, who let me borrow her salon and use her as a template for Claire. Denise, the reality of you makes any fictional character pale in comparison. So as great as Claire is, you are a hundred times better.

Thanks also to the Timians, for food, friendship, NASCAR and the use of their back room. (Which I'm telling you people is the coolest writing space I've ever been in.)

Chapter One

I haven't had a lot of experience with diapers, but I do know that you don't usually find them taped to dead men's chests. I'm Bella Bree MacGowan, and while I'm happy to report strange happenings like this in the *Royalton Star Weekly*, I would have passed on the early morning haircut if I knew I was going to be present at the discovery of the diapered dead dude. But there he was on the floor of my favorite hair salon, Planet Hair.

"What in the world?" Claire, Planet Hair's owner and stylist extraordinaire, froze midstride in the doorway. I gently pushed past her and realized I should have stayed outside. A middle-aged man in a mismatched suit was face up on the floor. I don't suppose there are many places dead men look at home, but surrounded by marigold walls and purple trim, it was like finding a corpse on a merry-go-round.

I knelt down and put my fingers to his neck, searching for a pulse. I'd felt skin like this before, cold and kind of... well, *dead*... and this guy's heart hadn't been pumping for a while. His dress shirt wasn't buttoned all the way up and as much as I didn't want to look at this guy I couldn't help but see there was something unusual on his chest. There was a line of grey silver duct tape and under that, a row of line-art duckies. I'd seen ducks like that before—on my cousin's infant. It was a diaper. I got an instant case of the creeps running up my spine.

I looked up at Claire and shook my head.

"There's a dead guy in my salon? Shit." Claire is a tough chick, but finding a body can shake a person up.

"We need to get out of here." I shooed her out the door and dragged my cell phone from my pocket.

I didn't dial 911. My best friend's husband, Tom Maverick, was the Commander of the Vermont State Police Barracks in Bethel, Vermont. I called him directly and let him sort it out. After Tom I called Randy, the photographer we used for the *Royalton Star*.

"Dead body at Planet Hair. Get over here now."

God help me, a little shiver of excitement ran through me. If I had anything to do with it, the paper would come out tomorrow morning with a shot of the dead guy on the front page. A scoop for the paper would be excellent. On the other hand, my stomach was starting to clench. Dead bodies had a way of wrecking my life.

Claire and I waited out on the covered sidewalk in the humidity. My leg was jiggling with nervous energy as I willed Randy to get here before the police. I was sweating even though it was only eight-thirty and we were standing in the shade. Claire looked at her watch, glanced back into the salon and then gazed at me with her eyebrows raised.

"You'd better call your clients, this is going to take all day," I said.

"My appointment book is in there with the dead guy." Claire frowned.

"Sorry."

It was fifteen minutes before two state police cruisers pulled up alongside the building. There were no lights or sirens. This was what I liked about Tom; he kept the fanfare at a minimum. Tom tended to be a low-key kind of guy, for a cop. He extracted himself from the first car and came over to me, while Officer Steve Leftsky and his partner hopped up onto the boardwalk and disappeared into the salon. Tom sat on the top step next to me.

"I should have known you'd be here. We've had two bodies in the past five years and you've found both of them."

"Three. You forgot Lily Wallace in California." Not that I wanted to remember the blood mingling with her hair in the river, but seeing a body fall from one of the tallest bridges in the United States isn't something you forget in a hurry.

"That's right. Body number three. You holding together?"

"I'm fine. At least there wasn't any blood this time. Could have been a natural death for all I know."

"Yeah. Not likely."

At the bottom of the stairs Claire waylaid a blond woman in her mid-fifties and led her to the other side of the road, next to the railroad tracks. I guessed it must be her next hair appointment—a dye job, if the dark streak in her part was any indication. The blonde left and Claire walked over to us.

"Any chance I can have my appointment book, Tom? I need to call people." Her voice was strong but her hands were shaking as she brushed a strand of dark-honey hair from her face. She attempted to slide it into her clip. It came loose immediately, surprising me. Claire's fingers were usually magic with hair.

"Hang on for a minute. I'll have Steve bring it out to you."

The medical examiner pulled up in his pickup,

followed by an ambulance. The EMTs waited in the ambulance while the ME headed our way. He nodded to Tom as he passed us and entered the salon.

"Going in?" I asked, still watching for Randy to show up.

"It can wait. That guy isn't going anywhere." Tom took off his hat and ran his hand across his head. He wore his hair old school military, so short he was practically bald. "What was our boy doing in Planet Hair? Stealing scissors? Any sign of a break in?"

"No. The door was locked, no broken windows, just the guy on the floor."

"Captain?" One of the officers stood in the doorway behind us. "You might want to see this."

Tom stood and I followed suit. Randy might not get here to take real photos but I could take a cell phone shot. Tom stood just inside the door and I peered around his shoulder. The medical examiner had the dead guy's shirt open all the way, the duct tape on his chest clearly holding down a diaper. I'd been right. I pulled out my cell phone, keeping it low and out of Tom's line of sight, but Randy arrived and pushed past me clicking pictures.

"What's he doing in here?" Tom blocked the camera with his arm but Randy dodged and snapped a couple more.

"Out!" Tom's face was turning purple. "Bree, you should know better."

Randy turned to go. "I got it. Check your email in thirty." A grin snaked across his face. "And don't let Tom give you a hard time."

"I said *out!*" The back of Tom's neck was bright red.

"I'm going. Don't get your boxers in a bunch."

Randy winked at me and went outside. I could see him through the window snapping pictures of the ambulance. He'd be ready when they wheeled the body out.

"What the hell is that?" Tom asked. "Silver duct tape on a man makes me think of explosives."

"Not explosives, Tom, you can relax. It's a diaper." The ME poked the soggy red diaper. "Full of blood."

I turned away. I knew from experience that blood has an adverse effect on my stomach. I heard someone retch and looked to see Claire behind me.

"Bree, get her out of here," Tom barked at me.

"No. I need to see this."

"I'm fine," Claire said, and then gagged again.

"Bree!"

"Tom! It's my job."

"My God. Be a human being for five minutes, Claire needs help."

"Shit. All right, I'm going, but only because blood makes me barf."

I found Claire standing on the stairs and led her away from the shop.

"Sorry," she said. "I didn't mean to mess up your story."

"I'll hunt down Tom later."

We walked around the corner away from the scene of the crime, even though I was dying to be there. Claire was looking a little less green away from the salon but I thought it would be a good idea to stay out of there until the body had been hauled away. I had more experience with dead bodies than she did. Hell, I had more experience with dead bodies than anyone I knew, besides Tom. A distinction I could do without, by the way.

Claire and I walked around the corner to the café situated under the *Royalton Star's* upstairs offices halfway down the block. We sat at the table in the front window where we could watch the comings and goings of the town. I wrangled the seat facing the street; I wanted to be able to see when the ambulance went by, and I didn't want Claire reminded of what she'd seen in her salon.

The Muffin Man, Dave, was waiting tables. Here was a man guaranteed to raise anyone's spirits. He squatted down next to Claire and fixed her with his hazel peepers and the color returned to her face.

"Looking good today, ladies. What can I get you?" He flashed his smile. I smiled back, feeling like I was back in high school.

We ordered coffee and the café's famous pumpkin and chocolate chip muffins and watched The Muffin Man walking back to the kitchen. I caught Claire's eye and we both giggled.

"Love the view in here," she said.

"Never fails to inspire. We are so high school."

"Thank God. If that didn't take me back to high school I'd start thinking I was getting old."

We got another smile from Dave when he brought our food. Claire had the good grace to blush and I figured I'd done my superhero duty for the day. But the story was niggling at my brain and I wanted to ask her about the guy, which was guaranteed to ruin the mood.

The door to the café slammed and I looked over to see Meg, my best friend/boss *and* Tom's wife, heading toward us. She squeezed behind me and banged the chair against the wall as she sat.

"Shouldn't you be upstairs writing this up?" she asked. "Or didn't you know there was a dead body in Planet Hair? Wait. Don't tell me. *You* found the body in

Planet Hair."

I nodded. "Claire and I walked in and there he was."

"I can't tell you how happy it makes me to have a reporter who finds things like bodies. But why aren't you upstairs getting this ready for tomorrow's paper?"

"I'm about to grill Claire, but I was trying to be tactful about it," I said, widening my eyes hoping she'd get my telepathic *don't spook my source*. "Let her get used to the idea of a dead body in her salon before starting in with the questions. Randy's got pictures."

"No point in grilling me anyway, I don't know who he was or what he's doing in my shop." Claire shrugged.

"See?" Meg said. "Get your butt upstairs."

"Don't you ever release news early? You could break this on the web," Claire said.

"We're the last paper on earth not to have an online edition," I said, looking pointedly at Meg.

"I'm not adding an online version until I figure out how it will benefit us," Meg said. "It's a whole... different level of advertising. I'd have to hire somebody to oversee the thing. It would cost us money."

"Wouldn't need to," Claire said, "You should talk to the editor of the Braintree paper. I do his hair. He's got a handle on the dual edition thing."

"I'll add it to my list." What she really meant was, *when pigs fly*. Meg hated the internet. About the time e-book sales and online news had started pushing out print editions she'd decided it was a zombie plot.

I pushed my chair back. "I've got to go to work." I turned to Claire. "What are you going to do about your clients?"

"Can I borrow your kitchen?" Claire asked Meg. Claire had worked out of her own kitchen for years before buying the salon, but since then she'd moved into the hills so her kitchen wasn't really an option anymore.

"Sure. Why not? It's not locked, but yell when you go in or Jeremy might come down in his underwear and embarrass himself."

"Thanks Meg." Claire leaned over and gave Meg a hug. "Thank God I've got my emergency make-over bag in the car."

Claire waved as she went out the door, and I stood up, tossing a couple of dollars on the table.

"Coming?"

"Go ahead up," Meg said. "I'll be up in a minute."

I climbed up to our second floor office. I was balancing my take-out coffee and raspberry chocolate chip muffin—I never could eat just one muffin. It was obvious Meg had already been up, the door was unlocked and the radio was on. I opened the window, sat down and powered up my computer. I set aside the notes for the story I had been planning to run and started typing, a thrill of glee running through me.

Deirdre, our paste-up tech, came in and shut the door softly. "Hey Bree. I won't chat; I know you're trying to finish that article."

"Actually, we've got a new front page. Large photo front and center as soon as Randy sends it over. I'm working on the article now."

Good to her word, Deirdre powered up her

computer and worked in silence. Deirdre looked meek, mild and slightly intimidated by life. She kept her strawberry hair clipped back and wore knee length skirts and twin sets. She also didn't say much, but she had the publishing software beaten into submission and when she did talk you never knew what would come out of her mouth. She knew highly technical computer terminology. And she could, and did, cuss worse than any road crew guy I knew.

I'd gotten down everything I could remember when Meg came flying in the door.

"There's a car in the lake! I heard it on the scanner." She was gesturing at me with her hands. "Quick! Go now and you'll be there when they pull it out."

"A car in the lake?" I was confused. I had a murder to investigate and Meg was waving her hands in the air over a submerged car.

"Call Randy and go. No. I'll call Randy, you go. Now!" She was practically jumping up and down.

"You call the shots," I said, and got out of my chair, wondering if she'd had a blow to the head.

"Bree! It's out-of-state plates! It could be the murderer's car. Go, go, go!" Meg was practically vibrating with energy.

"You think the car is connected to the murder? That's kind of a stretch don't you think?" I would have plopped myself back in the chair, but it would have given her a coronary.

"There's stuff floating above it. Diapers, ammunition!" Meg opened the door. "For the love of Pete, go!

I went, picking up my smallest dog, Annie the Beagle cross, on the way, even though I couldn't see how ammunition and diapers could be floating above the car. At least those objects made sense to me in relation to the murder.

Twenty minutes later, I was in Barnard, standing with my dog in a small crowd of people gazing into the lake. Sure enough, there was a car, and floating along the bank were a couple of empty boxes of shells and an empty bag of Ducky Diapers. Hot damn. I walked along the spillway and looked at the other bits of detritus floating there. Fast food wrappers, and napkins mostly. Nothing that looked relevant.

Randy showed up and went to work taking pictures. I left him to it, and sat on a bench with Beagle Annie at my knee waiting for the tow truck to show up. State Troopers were keeping an eye on the onlookers and I was scratching Beagle Annie's head, telling her that they should send the children home before the tow truck got there, because God knew what might be in the car. Sure enough, when the wrecker finally showed up the troopers moved everyone across the street. They let Randy and I stay—it was the advantage of being with the press.

There was some argument about who was going into the water to hook up the car. The truck driver felt that there should be a dive crew there to take care of it, and the troopers hadn't called and didn't want to wait for them to show up. In the end, one of the troopers pulled off everything but his pants and walked the cable out as far as he could. He swam over the vehicle and dove down. I was antsy. The thought of having to hold your breath while trying to hook a cable to a submerged car gave me palpitations. I let out my breath when he surfaced and gave the winch operator the thumbs up. The winch pulled in the slack and the line went taut.

The noise was deafening and I held my hands over Beagle Annie's ears as a white Ford Taurus with New York plates was pulled up and sucked out of the water. When all four tires were on the bank and the car was unhooked those of us who could gathered close, while the civilians were kept on the other side of the road.

I took a deep breath and steeled myself for the worst as a trooper opened the door and the lake rushed out. No bodies, thank God. Randy was moving around taking pictures through the windows, but there wasn't much to see. There were some wrappers that hadn't floated out, and a river rock on the gas pedal. Someone popped the trunk and we looked in at a couple of suitcases, correction, a suitcase and a rifle case - the Trooper had popped it open and it wasn't even damp. I immediately thought of fingerprints. The rifle case was snapped shut and tagged, along with the suitcase. The car was pulled up onto the tow truck and the show was over.

I walked over to the trooper who had toweled off and redressed, he was tying his regulation black shoes and hadn't left with the other cruisers. Beagle Annie stuck out her ears like flags, making her look like she knew something we didn't, and focused her black rimmed eyes on the Trooper.

"Did you get a look at that rifle?" I asked him.

He looked up at me. "Yeah. Why?" He finished with his laces and stood, he was a good ten inches taller than me.

"There was something different about it, I wondered if you knew what it was?" I crossed my fingers that he'd talk to me; otherwise I'd be searching Google images all afternoon.

"It had a silencer on it." He reached down to pat

Beagle Annie and then straightened to put his hat on his head. She looked a little put out and I could tell she'd been just about to roll onto her back for a tummy rub.

"Isn't that kind of unusual?" I had no idea if it was unusual or not, but I was hoping he'd tell me.

"Not much use for a silencer when you're hunting in the woods. Take care." He touched the brim of his hat and headed for his cruiser.

Where do you hunt if you aren't hunting in the woods? The city? There's only one kind of prey in the city. If you don't count the rats.

I was at my desk with Beagle Annie under my feet, trying to figure out the connection between the murder and the car when Lucy Howe blew in the door. Beagle Annie growled low in her throat and my bitch-o-meter kicked on, but she wrote for the paper on occasion so I did my best to play nice.

"Lucy." I smiled but my face felt like plastic.

"Bree." Lucy didn't look any more sincere than I felt. "I hear there was a murder in town. Care to share?"

"News travels fast." Way faster than I anticipated. Beagle Annie growled again, I hushed her.

"It pays to have connections. Randy told me." She smiled her superior *I know how to get information out of people and you don't* smile.

"I didn't know you and Randy were close." *And poor Randy if you are.*

"I extended him a few favors, so he extends me

some." She shrugged.

Ew.

"We already have a front page spread on the dead guy, sorry," I said.

"It's not for Meg. I've been engaged by the Valley News. They liked the idea of a local reporting on the story. And since The Star is a weekly and the News is a daily I'm going to be able to report more, sooner." She left off the *nyah, nyah, nyah nyah nyah*, but it was implied.

"You'd better talk to Tom then. I'm sure you don't want second hand news from me." I turned back to my keyboard. Beagle Annie's low growls were vibrating on my foot, but Lucy couldn't hear her.

"You found the body. Nothing second hand about that. But if you won't talk I can always go see Claire. I need a haircut." She turned and left, the stink of her narcissistic superiority following after her.

I picked up the phone.

"Claire. Lucy Howe is headed your way. I'd really appreciate it if you didn't say much." I was tapping my fingers on my desk top, wondering how to beat Lucy at her own game.

"She was here an hour ago. I didn't tell her anything she wouldn't have heard on the street."

I should have known. I would have preferred that she not say anything at all, but I guess that was asking a little too much.

Next I called Randy to warn him that Lucy might show up, but I was too late there too, he'd given her a flash drive and I was willing to bet she wasn't bringing that flash drive to me. I'd be surprised if they didn't show up in tomorrow's big daily paper.

"Then get it back! Those are my pictures."

"But Lucy said…"

"Lucy didn't hire you, I did!"

I slammed down the phone. "Fuck!" I put all the suppressed rage I could muster into the word.

Deirdre walked into the office while I was swearing.

"Sorry, Deirdre."

"I take it things aren't going well."

"I've got it handled." *I hope.*

I got back on the phone to the Barracks and started nagging Steve Leftsky for information on the Murder.

"Didn't I just talk to you? I've got work to do." I thought he was kidding around, but he could have been truly exasperated with me. I couldn't tell over the phone.

"It's been at least twenty-four hours. I'm working on the murder, now. Different article, different legal pad, different phone call. Even a different pen in my mouth. And I was giving you a break, so spill." I was trying to train myself to keep my pen out of my mouth when I was on the phone, but it wasn't working out for me.

"Bree, I just don't know anything."

"Was there ID?" I asked, wondering if Tom had asked the guys to keep their mouths closed.

"Look. There was nothing. We've got a dead John Doe dressed in mismatched clothes with a hole in his chest. That's it. Nothing else."

"But he wasn't killed at the salon, was he?" That was pretty clear from the lack of blood but I wanted to hear him say it. I'd read *Investigative Reporting for Dummies.*

"You were there, what did you see?"

"No blood." I thought of the soggy red diaper and shuddered.

"You can deduce something from that can't you?

I hung up and wrote the piece, which didn't take long because there wasn't anything to say except *Hey everybody, there was a dead guy at Planet Hair!* I zapped it over to Deirdre for her to set and started thinking about next week's article before coming to my senses.

"We'd better get the paper put together."

Chapter Two

The paper went together easily, so while I liked to help, I wasn't really necessary. I'd been the paste-up tech from the beginning of the paper until Meg promoted me to reporter, but I'd never been as good at it as Deirdre. She was the queen. Consequently, we were done way before our midnight deadline, and I was driving home in time to feed my animals. I was still fuming over Lucy Howe. I wanted to break this story. Not the tiny piece that would appear in our paper tomorrow, but the whole shebang. An article like that, done right, could get me noticed, give me options. I'm not saying I would leave my little town to work at a big city daily, but it would be nice to have the choice.

My truck made interesting noises all the way home and blew out black smoke when I pulled into the drive and turned it off. Damn. I was going to have to take a second job again. I sighed and let Beagle Annie out. The rest of my gaggle of dogs ran around the house to meet me. Annabelle Cat was stretched out on the porch railing, pretending it wasn't taking every ounce of her considerable concentration to keep her from falling off. I was up to five dogs, including Beans. Technically, Beans was not my dog. He belonged to my last boyfriend, Beau. The conversation we'd had when we broke up went something like this:

Me: "You can't expect me to continue to take care of Beans when you go out of town. He's your responsibility." *Damn it!*

Beau: "I only took that dog because you wanted him."

Me: "I didn't ask you to take in Beans."

Beau: "But I knew you wanted him."

Me: "I already have four dogs. I did not need another one. I told you that. Beans is your dog and you need to take care of him." *When you break up with a girl, you need to have some common courtesy and not keep showing up at her house.*

Beau: "Everything would have been fine if you hadn't turned into that woman that's always finding dead bodies."

Me: "What are you talking about?" *You think I want to find dead bodies?*

Beau: "You know, that girl in the books who's always finding dead bodies."

Me: "You're changing the subject."

Beau: "Obviously."

Me: "I am not that dead body girl." *Oh God. I'm the dead body girl.*

And then, the first time he had to go out of town, he'd left Beans home alone at his house with food and water and called me from the plane to ask if I'd check in on the little Chihuahua. Beans had been living with me ever since. And I'd gotten him a tag with my address in case he got lost. But he was *not* my dog. However, I treated him like my dog. It only seemed fair.

The dogs followed me into the barn to feed my pony and Max's horses. Max is a supposed-to-be-retired farmer who lives up the hill from me with his wife, Mary. Only he hates not working. He keeps his horses on my farm and we trade off chores. He keeps an eye on the farm when I'm at work, and if the animals get out he rounds them up. It's a good partnership and I don't ever come home to discover my animals in someone else's vegetable garden. I can't tell you how comforting that is.

I fed the bunnies and noticed the chickens' grain was getting low. I really should be charging my neighbors for eggs, organic feed is not cheap. Stripes, the skunk that thought he was a dog, was hanging around outside the chicken fence.

"No eggs for you," I told him. "I put your tuna in the storm drain."

Stripes followed me to the house, which still made me kind of nervous. He hadn't sprayed in a long time, but the potential was still there. Diesel, the boxer ran over to Stripes, they sniffed noses and Diesel rolled the skunk over and snuffled his belly. Thank God skunks can't spray when they're on their backs.

Annabelle Cat hopped down from the porch rail as I came up the stairs and followed me into the house with the other dogs. I inherited my house from my grandma. My brothers got money, which made them happy, and I got the farm, which made me happy. I'd done a little remodeling, mostly putting in a bunch more windows, painting walls and tossing a bunch of furniture.

I grabbed a Greek yogurt with honey from the fridge and ate it leaning with my back to the sink. I'm great at compartmentalizing but now that my chores for the day were done, the body in Planet Hair was on my mind.

It was just so unlikely. Why dump a body there? I could see the benefits; Planet Hair was situated out of the line of site from the Green, the New England equivalent of the town square. Because Planet Hair was at the end of the building and the porch didn't extend past the door, no one could glance in and see the body. But still, it didn't make sense to me.

I set aside the body as 'unanswered questions' and rooted around in the fridge for something else to eat. I grabbed an apple and a soda, heading to the living room to hang out on my couch. I truly did mean to watch TV, go to bed and forget about the murder, but questions kept cropping up in my mind. Like, why diapers? And why not just dump the body in the river? So I turned on the lamp, got a pad of paper and a pen, and started taking notes. I'd find the facts if it killed me.

There are certain perks to working over the main drag in town. Food is one of them. Unfortunately, when I walked into the café to pick up my grilled cheese sandwich and a cup of tomato soup, I spotted the front cover of the *Valley News*. While I was waiting I bought the paper and opened the *News* and placed it on the counter next *to The Star*. My article had more detail than Lucy's, and thankfully Randy hadn't signed a release for the *News*, so we had the only photos of the dead body, but when it came to actual facts they were identical. Crap.

When I finally climbed the stairs to the office, there was a woman standing on the landing outside our door. She was petite, slim and wearing a coat that clearly came off a New York runway. I instantly morphed into an over-sized Vermont woodchuck. Which I was, and proud of it, but there's nothing like coming face to face with your polar opposite to make you aware of your weak points. Her dark hair was cut short, the ends of her bob sweeping her cheeks when she turned to look at me coming up the stairs.

I balanced my sandwich on the cup of soup and unlocked the door. She followed me in, looking around the office as if it had a sour smell.

"Can I help you?" I asked, wondering what the hell she was doing here. "I'm afraid Meg isn't in today, but I can take the information if you want an ad."

She looked at me strangely. I flashed back to high school when I'd said the principal was an old cow and discovered her standing directly behind me. Not a good sign. But the woman smiled and held out her hand.

"I am Michèle Ledroit." She had a distinct European accent. "This is a news agency? Am I correct?"

"Yes. *The Royalton Star.*" What was she after? I gestured to the chairs at my desk. "Would you like to sit down?"

"Thank you." She sat upright in the chair, her ankles crossed, prim in contrast to Tom's comfortable sprawl of yesterday.

"How can I help you?" I was all curiosity. This woman was clearly out of her element, and strangers don't just wander in to our offices. You kind of have to want to find us to get here.

"I am looking for a man, my boyfriend, named Victor Puccini." Her bottom lip trembled.

"Victor Puccini? I'm sorry, I've never heard of him? You thought he was here? At the paper?" Could this be another story brewing? First a murder, then a submerged car, now a missing Italian. This was turning out to be a good week.

"Not here specifically, but I think the car that was found in the lake was his." Tears gleamed at the corners of her eyes.

"The white Taurus was Victor Puccini's?" *That's interesting.* What were the chances the three incidents were related?

"I'm sorry, I really am but I don't know what I can do for you. Have you talked to the police?"

"They don't know anything at all." The tears trickled down her face and she blotted them with the back of her hand.

I handed her my box of tissues. "You must know a man was found murdered here as well. Not to be indelicate, but could it have been your boyfriend?"

"It wasn't him. They showed me a picture, and it wasn't him but I don't know where he is." She wiped her nose and took another tissue. "He must here somewhere."

"I wish I could help you, but I don't know what I can do. I'm a reporter, not a detective."

"Could you just keep your eyes open? You might see someone you don't recognize... You could tell me?" She handed me a card. "This is my number."

"Where are you from?" I asked. There was a phone number on the card, and her name, Michèle Ledroit, but nothing else.

"I am originally from Paris, but I am currently living in New York City. Victor was expected home a few days ago and did not return."

"Victor Puccini," I said. "I can keep him in mind, but I can't guarantee anything."

"Call me if you find him." She stood and looked down at me. "There is a reward."

"Just out of curiosity, what made you come to me? Why not a private detective?" I dropped my gaze to the business card, considered picking it up, but let it lie.

"I was asking in the general store about getting help and they said 'Bree MacGowan'. Then in the cafe downstairs, again it was 'Bree MacGowan'. The post mistress said you were nosy, so then I knew I had the right person to ask." She looked me in the eye. "It is an insult to be called 'nosy,' no? But today it is the highest compliment."

Great. I'd been insulted by half the town and a Parisian waterworks.

Ledroit left, and I called Steve Leftsky to see if I could get an ID on the New York plates.

"I don't know, Bree. I'm not sure Tom would be happy with me feeding you information," he said.

"For God sake, Steve, I can get it off the internet if I have to. Can't you just give me the information?" I was pretty sure I could run plates, but I didn't want to pay the fee.

"Margaret LeDonne." He sighed. "She's been notified and the insurance is taking care of the details."

"Thanks, Steve. You're a prince. I owe you one." I was scribbling the details onto my legal pad.

"And we both know I'll never collect."

I was accumulating names. The interesting thing was that Margaret LeDonne and Victor Puccini were both Italian. Michèle Ledroit was French. And yet Ledroit was connected to Puccini. *Interesting.*

I ate my lunch while I considered Michèle Ledroit. I didn't quite know what to make of her. She was elegant but not what I would call warm or friendly. She cried over her boyfriend but somehow she seemed distant. I picked up her card and flipped it over. On the

23

back she had written *$1000 reward for the location of Victor Puccini, $500 reward for information instrumental in his recovery.*

I would keep my eyes open.

Identity of body found at Planet Hair was as far as I'd gotten on the follow-up article when Tom walked in followed by a tall man with a shaved head. The guy's bulging, tattooed biceps looked familiar. I couldn't see his face, but the butterflies in my stomach were a good indication that my intuition was right. He turned from closing the door and I was face to face with Richard Hambecker.

My feelings about Hambecker were conflicted. He'd abducted me from my home the previous winter, but only so he wouldn't blow his cover. I'd poisoned him to get away, so maybe that made us even. I'd say he didn't play well with others, except sometimes he did. And if I was telling the truth, I'd say there was a certain attraction between us.

He smiled a slow smile and heat began to build in my midsection. I felt a smile start to form and squashed it. I didn't know if I should hit him or throw my arms around him. But my first instinct was to hit him.

"What the hell is he doing here?" I asked Tom.

"I thought you said she'd be glad to see you," Tom said, turning to Hambecker.

"I think what I actually said was that Bree would be *excited* to see me." Hambecker looked me over. "She looks pretty excited."

"Excuse me," I said. "I'm sitting right here. You have a lot of nerve bringing him here."

"I take it you didn't part on good terms?" Tom pulled out one of the chairs from the front of my desk.

"Part on good terms?" I was spluttering. "We didn't *part*. We were in the middle of a firefight, and he and Moose just disappeared. Never to be seen again, apparently. Until today."

"It wasn't really a firefight, you know. No shots fired. More like a Mexican Standoff." There wasn't an iota of tension in Hamecker's body. Not a twitch, a clench or a tick to show he had any feelings at all seeing me again.

I stood up and looked at him, my eyes narrowing. "The point is, you vanished. It was your doing I was there in the first place. Anything could have happened at that point, and you bugged out. You left me there."

"And here you are safe and sound. I had no doubts about your ability to take care of yourself; it was a full time job keeping you contained." Hambecker leaned against the wall not far from me, giving me the eye.

My face was hot. My ears could combust at any minute, and I was momentarily tongue-tied. Deirdre took advantage of the silence and grabbed her purse. "If Meg comes in tell her I'll be back in half an hour, will you? I have a feeling you don't need me around for this."

I nodded and moved back to my chair. The trouble with this arrangement was that Hambecker was effectively out of my line of sight. I could see him only if I swiveled my chair or turned my head to look directly at him. I was pretty sure he did that on purpose. I turned my attention to Tom, trying to convince myself that I didn't care where Hambecker was.

Tom leaned back, stretching his legs out to the side of my workspace. There wasn't any tension in him either, and I might have relaxed if it wasn't for the knowledge that Hambecker was behind me.

Tom pulled a voice recorder from his pocket and put it on my desk. "MacGowan, I want you to walk us through what happened yesterday. Go slow; give us as much detail as you can."

I turned to look at Hambecker. His face was unreadable. I found that incredibly annoying.

"You never did say why Hambecker is here."

A ghost of a smile appeared at the corners of his mouth. "I'm consulting."

I raised my eyebrows.

"The dead guy is a person of interest."

"Who is, uh, *was* he?" I asked.

"There's a possibility that this death is related to a case the Feds are working on. Richard is here to look into that." Tom looked like he had a stomach ache. "Can we get on with this?"

I nodded and took a breath, casting back. I started with the drive into town and took them through what I'd seen until Tom arrived at the salon. There wasn't much to tell since we hadn't been in the shop for more than a minute.

"I got gypped. I was supposed to get my hair cut."

"You made out better than the guy in the salon." I swear Tom was making an effort not to roll his eyes at me.

"Too true. That's it. I don't have anything else for you. Can I ask a question?"

"Fire away," Tom leaned back. "I don't promise I'll be able to answer it.

"Why'd he have a diaper taped to him?"

"We think they were transporting him and didn't want to leave a blood trail. He had one taped to his back too."

"That's gross. And weird. Did they happen to have diapers on hand, or did they have to go out and buy them? And did they think of that ahead of time and go out and buy them first or after the fact?" I narrowed my eyes. "Do you know who he is?" I threw the important question in at the end. With any luck it would be the easiest to answer, and Tom would tell me.

"All good questions," Tom said. "But I suggest you leave those questions to us. You'll be giving yourself nightmares."

I snorted. "If finding the other two bodies didn't give me nightmares then this won't. There wasn't even any blood on the ground." Compared to the other two bodies I'd found a balding man in a bad suit with diapers taped to him was almost pleasant.

"Whatever you say," Tom said. "But I happen to know you aren't as tough as you think you are." He stood up. "We'll call you if we need anything else."

"Don't you need me to sign a statement or something?" I knew a bit about cops; they always made you sign things.

"I'll get this typed up and bring it by for you to sign. No need for you to drive down to the barracks. My wife would kill me if I pulled you away from the office during paste up." Tom smiled. "Where is she, by the way? She's usually here by now."

"Last I saw her she was at the coffee shop." I indicated the restaurant below us. "Hang on. You're going to type that up? Isn't that a little below the status of the Captain of the barracks?"

27

"When I said 'I'll get this typed up,' what I meant was I'll have an admin type it up. I wasn't planning on doing it myself." He moved toward the door. "I think I'll have Vicki do it, she's fast."

"Come on Tom, give me something here. Was the dead guy from here?" Just because I'd never seen him alive didn't mean he hadn't lived around here somewhere. "Why was he dressed in clothes that didn't fit him?"

Tom shrugged. "Couldn't tell you." He finished his sentence as he started down the stairs and I heard the lower door bang shut as the left building.

I turned to Hambecker, who was still leaning against the window-sill. A moth was beating its wings against the window.

"Do *you* know who he is?" I asked.

"I heard you were instrumental in apprehending the Senator. Nice work." Hambecker caught the moth in his hand, opened the window and let it fly away.

"You aren't going to answer me, are you?"

"I think you just missed the part where I complimented you."

"Thank you. But it was really Stripes. If he hadn't shown up I'd probably be dead."

"The skunk? I doubt it."

"Who's Stripes? Did you add a zebra to your menagerie since I was there? he asked.

"Stripes is a skunk." I said. "Duh." I wasn't feeling especially mature.

"Saved by a skunk. I would have never guessed." He pushed himself upright. "See you around, Trouble." He tapped his knuckles on the desk as he walked past.

"Considering that you were the cause…" But he was gone. I caught a glimpse of a six inch rip in his jeans just below his left butt cheek and the door slammed behind him. Just one Richard Hambecker sighting had caused my hands to start sweating, and my stupid heart was beating faster just seeing him again. He was excellent to look at and totally bad news.

Chapter Three

Thursday morning, when my egg, sausage and cheese sandwich was reduced to crumbs on my desk, my coffee cup was three quarters empty and Beagle Annie was once again asleep under my desk, I booted my computer and scanned the list of articles I was planning. Good stuff, but not what I was going to write about this week. I picked up the phone.

"Bree." Tom's voice was warm. Not too much stress today. Good.

"What can you tell me about the guy in Planet Hair, Maverick?" I was doodling on my legal pad and wishing I had more coffee. I needed my brain to be sharp.

"This again? Lucky you have me in your pocket, MacGowan. Anyone else would have fed this to the *Valley News* just to get you off their back." His chair creaked.

"One of life's perks. So what's the deal?" I dropped my pen on the desk and leaned back, resting my heels on the desk.

"I don't have any more details. We don't have an ID. We don't have a motive. We've got bupkis." He was more matter of fact rather than upset. "But we should have a fingerprint match today, dental records tomorrow or the next day. Give us a couple of days with the car, and before you know it we'll have a case.

"Come on! You've got to have something to give

me." *I* was upset.

"Nope. Investigation's stalled until forensics come back." Tom said. Still no hint of frustration.

"That's bull." They had to have something by now. They had Hambecker here for cripes sake. "Did Hambecker take over the investigation?" I could see that happening.

"Nope. He has bigger fish to fry. Unless there's an issue we don't know about, he wouldn't have jurisdiction."

Oh, yeah. Jurisdiction. That was always important.

"Do we know if the car from the lake is related to the murder?" I was trying to cover all the angles like the big boys do.

"Nothing definitive."

"What about the rifle?" *Come on. There has to be a connection.* I felt like I should be blowing on dice.

"It takes time, Bree." He let out a sigh. I was ruining his mood.

"Come *on*, Tom!" You'd never know I was his wife's best friend. "What about time of death, do you have that?"

"Right around 11P.M. That's the official word from the coroner."

"Well that's *something*." I jotted down the time. "But no suspects at all? Hambecker doesn't have any ideas?" I was pushing now.

"Not that I know of." He rang off with the excuse of work. More like he'd had more than enough of me.

Bupkis was right. *Dang.* What could I do with time of death? Bupkis.

"Hey you," Meg said as she came in the door, "I thought you were coming over to the house last night. You forget?" Meg threw her bag onto the shelf behind her desk. "We need to talk about next week's front page."

"I'm working on it now. Headline: *Identity of body found at Planet Hair*, and then either *still a mystery*, or *is revealed*. With a photo of Claire in front of her salon. What do you think?"

"You could put a picture of Claire naked on the cover for all I care. Just as long as it sells papers."

"Is circulation down?" I said.

"No, but someone is telling our advertisers it is. Tireless Tractors and Steadfast Feeds are threatening to pull their ads. If they go, others will follow."

"That's crap. Who told them our numbers were down?" My sixth sense was pointing straight at Lucy Howe.

"Don't know, and no one is talking."

"Maybe we should launch an Internet edition. Tell them that we'll throw in online ads for free for the first month or so."

"I can't see that doing anything for us. How's it going to increase revenue? More to the point, how can we prove that people are seeing their ads?"

"Run a coupon. Tag it so they can tell when people print it off the Internet and bring it in."

"I don't know Bree, we already have a cash flow problem, how can I pay someone to oversee the online edition?"

"I'll do it for free until it gets off the ground." Just what I needed, more work for the same pay.

"I'll think about it. But don't push me, okay. You know how I feel about the Internet." She went to her desk and dumped her purse.

I did know. Meg resented the rate at which electronic data was supplanting print media. Paper was everything; it was tradition with a capital T.

"Do you think I should take some night classes in investigative reporting?" As much as I didn't want to be insecure about my reporting skills, I was.

"I don't think you need to, at least not for me, but if you want to then go for it. I'm all for self-improvement. In others. You won't catch me going back to school."

"That's kind of a non-answer: sure, but I wouldn't?"

"You're doing a fine job for a small time paper. I don't want to lose you, but if you see a future at a big city paper someday, then you probably should. It's been eight years since you graduated, and I don't know, did you take classes in journalism?" I guess I hadn't talked much about school with Meg.

"Yeah. A couple. Nothing hardcore." And I hadn't paid attention. What does a small town farm girl need with a degree in business and journalism? I don't know what I thought I was going to do when I graduated.

"Do what you need to do. But do it for yourself, not for me." She focused her attention on her computer. "And make sure it doesn't interfere with your day job."

I was getting hungry, and a glance out the window told me the fire department had fired up the big grill on the green. "Going to eat chicken at Old Home Days?"

Old Home Days is a Vermont—or maybe a New England—thing. It's basically an excuse to eat too much food, drink too much beer and watch little kids ride rinky-dink carnival rides. Like a county fair on the opposite of steroids.

"I wish. I'm going to West Leb for office supplies this afternoon. You want to come?"

"Sure, as long as we're going to do lunch."

I wrote, and Meg talked to advertisers on the phone. Deirdre didn't work on Thursdays. There wasn't enough work for her to worry about being here. Besides she worked enough overtime on paste-up day that she could probably work a three-day work week and get more than enough hours.

Meg shut me down at noon. "Lunch," she said. "Let's go."

I deserted my article for the promise of food and put a bowl of water out for Beagle Annie, who lifted her head and looked at me with her dark brown, black-lined eyes, to see if she was invited. She put her head back down when I didn't call her. We locked the office and walked down the stairs to Meg's car. My ex-boyfriend once removed, James Fisk, was coming out of the coffee shop as we were getting into the Subaru. He was another guy who'd dumped me when my life got too complicated for him. I ducked my head and tried to hide. I wasn't fast enough. James raised his hand in greeting and came to stand next to my window. I rolled my eyes at Meg and lowered the window.

"Hi Jim."

"MacGowan. Meg." He nodded his head in Meg's direction. "Bree, I've got tickets to the NASCAR at Louden next weekend. Want to go?"

"Are you offering me the tickets?" I was being perverse. He wasn't offering me the tickets; he was asking me on a date. But I couldn't help busting his chops.

"Uh. No. I'm asking you if you'd like to go to the races with me." He spoke slowly and I could tell it was an effort for him not to roll his eyes.

"No. Thank you. I'm not available to go to the

races with. Gotta go."

"When are you going to stop punishing me for that mistake?"

I rolled up the window and Meg backed out of the parking spot, leaving Jim standing there with a scowl on his face.

"You know," I said, "he still has my house key."

"You never lock your door anyway."

"Yeah. But that's not the point. Him having my key is the point." The thought of keys rang bells in my head. Excitement buzzed through my body. "Wait. Do you mind if I bail on lunch?"

"Does this have to do with the murder?"

"Yeah. Drop me at your house. There's something I want to ask Claire."

Claire is nothing if not flexible. She'd set up shop in Meg's kitchen and was sitting in a straight back chair eating a sandwich and talking on the phone. She rang off when she saw me.

"My cleaning service," she said, cutting her eyes to the phone. "She wanted to know when she could get back in the salon."

"What did you tell her?"

"I have no clue. I don't even know when *I'm* getting back in the salon."

"Bad for business, huh?"

"No! The phone's been ringing nonstop. I don't know how word got out so quickly."

"Are you kidding? The phone tree has probably been buzzing since we found that guy. Half the people in this town have a police scanner." I leaned on the kitchen counter across from Claire.

"Do you want me to cut your hair? I scheduled myself some time for errands but I don't feel like going out." She pushed the last bite of her sandwich into her mouth and got up to wash her hands in the sink.

"Sure. If you don't mind answering some questions while you're cutting." I moved to the straight back chair. "What are you doing for clients that want their hair washed?" I asked.

"I have them lean over the sink. Meg's got one of those sprayers that slide out of the faucet. Do you want me to wash your hair?"

"Nah. I was just curious. I washed it this morning."

Claire picked up a spray bottle and started misting me down.

"What's on your mind?" she asked. She was pulling a comb through my damp hair. It's not that easy; I've got wavy, snarly hair that I don't comb often enough.

"To be blunt, I was wondering how many people have keys to your salon. The door wasn't forced, right?"

"I don't think so. It's pretty easy to wiggle the inner door open, but the outer door was locked."

"Who all has keys? Who could get in without anyone noticing?"

"Ronnie—that's Veronica Hart, my cleaning lady, she cleans like nobody's business, but she's developmentally disabled. Maybe autistic. She didn't kill the guy. Jim has a key. He still asks about you, you know. Gets his hair cut every four weeks and asks about you every time. Lori, the stylist who used to rent space from me, she still has a key." Claire stopped snipping for a moment. "That's it. I can't think of anyone else who might have a key. There might be someone from before I was here, but that was a long time ago. The place had been empty for a while when I moved in."

"Not a very likely list of killers. I was thinking it could be someone who had a key, but now I'm not so sure." I watched my hair hitting the ground. "You're sure you locked the door last night?"

"I locked it. Are *you* sure Jim is above bumping someone off?"

I laughed.

"Mr. Squeaky Clean? No, I can't see him doing that. He'd rather sue the pants off somebody than shoot a hole in them."

"Although…" Claire said, and then started to laugh.

"Although, what? Don't leave me in the dark here."

"Sorry. I just got a vision of Jim wanting to put this guy in his trunk, but he doesn't want to get blood on his car. So he runs in the pharmacy and buys a package of diapers and duct tape. And *then*, when he's got the guy all cleaned up and he's wrapped in duct tape and diapers he has to go to the thrift store and get some clothes to put on the body. And after all that, he can't get him in the trunk of his car because it's too small, and he sits him up in the passenger seat and drives around talking to him like he's still alive." She snorted with laughter.

"You got all that in a three-second vision?" Not that I was surprised, I could cook up a lot more than that in three seconds.

"Yeah. Good imagination huh?" She was sliding my hair straight up between her fingers and snipping the ends. I knew that's what was happening but it was strange not to have the big mirror so I could watch her face as we talked.

I thought it was pretty interesting that she could envision Jim being anything but a straight-laced if somewhat jerky upstanding citizen. It made me wonder would he kill someone if he got mad enough. "Do you think Jim would kill someone if he thought justice wasn't being served? Like if he knew some guy was guilty and he got off?"

"Mr. I-believe-in-the-processes-of-the-law? I don't know. If he knew beyond a doubt that someone had killed a child or something like that? It's possible, I guess. People get strange with they are obsessed with certain ideals." Claire was combing through my hair now.

"There's something else, though. I have a key to Planet Hair hidden, just in case I forget mine, or I'm driving Paul's car. Someone could have discovered it."

"Shit. That's screws up my line of inquiry." Anyone in the damn town could have found Claire's key.

"You're going to investigate? Tom wouldn't approve of that would he?" She came around to look at the front of my hair and looked me square in the eye. "You're not going to get yourself in trouble again are you? Because if you are, I want in."

"I'm just doing a little back story for my article. That's all. You can tag along if you want to." Although if Hambecker found out I'd dragged Claire into it he'd probably skin me alive.

"I have a better idea. I talk to people all day long; I bet I could find stuff out." She was flipping the ends of my hair with the curling iron, as if it wasn't a waste of time.

"You're on." I said.

"Are you coming to the bar tonight?" Claire asked. "Grant Fraser is going to be there."

"He must have won a race last weekend," I said.

"It was a big Formula 1 race, down south. He'll be buying drinks tonight. You should come."

With my hair sufficiently groomed into submission I walked the mile back into town. The day was warm, but not muggy, and a slight breeze was blowing through the valley. It felt good to walk once the stiffness worked itself out. Irises were blooming in flower gardens along the way. I felt light and happy. Endorphins; there had to be ways besides exercise to get them flowing.

Oh, yeah. Sex and chocolate. I already ate too much chocolate.

I had already decided to start with the key holders even though it was possible some unknown murderer could have gotten in to Claire's shop. Now I looked up Ronnie Hart's address. Later I'd interview Ronnie, but I thought I should do some looking around first. It wasn't like the murderer was going to come out and tell me they'd done it.

Ronnie's house was a small cape set back from the road a few minutes out of Tunbridge. I parked in a lay-by just past her property and tossed the Gala apple I'd been eating into the ditch. I slipped into the orchard adjacent to the hay fields surrounding the little farmhouse. It wasn't all that unusual for hikers to tromp over the Vermont landscape and I was betting on being able to pass unnoticed. As I came out from under the trees the sun hit me. It was a warm evening and the long grass swished along my thighs as I walked. I hoped I was loud enough to scare any snakes away, and put thoughts of ticks out of my head. There wasn't anything I could do about those suckers except pick them off later, and thinking about them gave me the shudders.

I'd looked for vehicles in the dooryard as I passed by. None. The absence of a vehicle didn't necessarily mean there wasn't anyone home, so I'd still need to stay alert. I walked through the hay until the shed hid me from view of the house and then I turned to approach it. I had no idea what I thought I was going to find, but hey, I was working on instinct.

There was a scorched area of dirt about twenty feet behind the out building. Kind of a strange spot for a burn pile, but I'd seen stranger. It looked recent; pieces of a blackened and soggy carpet lay on the edge of the area. But burning trash wasn't exactly unusual out here. I skirted the ash and came up on the rear of the building I peeked through the single window. It was dark, but the door was cracked open at the other end and I could see the silhouette of a man standing just inside.

I was pretty sure it was Richard Hambecker.

Chapter Four

I ducked out of sight and moved away from the window, standing with my back against the shed, my heart thudding in my chest. Crap. Crap and double crap. I sucked in air and willed my heart rate to slow. I had no interest in facing a Hambecker grilling, so snooping here could wait for another day. I practically tiptoed past the burn spot and headed back the way I came, walking fast and listening for footsteps behind me. I could practically feel the target on my back.

I felt a little better when I reached the cool shadows of the overgrown orchard, but I wasn't sure where I'd stepped into the trees and I didn't really want to walk the road where I could be easily spotted. I was debating which path to take through the trees when a hand fell on my shoulder, spun me around and I was face to face with one angry federal agent. I fixed him with my most innocent smile.

"What are you doing here?" Hambecker's tone was light but I could hear the edge in it. "Stay out of this, Bree. It's not your business." He dropped his hand from my shoulder and crossed his arms over his chest.

I stood for a moment, my feet in the soft mulch of decaying leaves, a breeze ruffling my hair. I couldn't believe I'd ever been attracted to this guy. Had he always been this obnoxious? I remembered him as a little pushy, but he was beyond annoying now. I mirrored his stance, arms crossed, back ramrod straight.

"Of course it's my business, I'm a reporter. You know about reporters, right? They report the news. That murder in the salon, Hammie? That's news."

"Don't call me Hammie." He narrowed his eyes at me. "And don't mess with a federal investigation. I won't hesitate to lock you up, Bree." He hit me with his best *don't think that I won't* face.

"Believe me, I've spent enough time handcuffed in your company to know what you're capable of. But this is my turf, Hammie, and it's not going to be easy to get me rotting in a cell. I've got friends." I could feel my throat constricting with anger, and I forced myself to relax. I wasn't about to let Richard Hambecker see me getting choked up. With my luck he'd think I was speechless over him. *As if.* I uncrossed my arms and stood with my hands on my hips.

Taking his cue from me, Hambecker relaxed his body and mirrored my stance. A light bulb popped in my head—he was using body language to get me to agree with him. Well, two could play at this game. I smiled even more sweetly and shifted my weight so one hip was jutting out.

"I can see your point," he said, and it was all I could do not to laugh, except that I also felt the draw. His voice was soft now, the edge and anger gone. I could practically see the wheels turning in his head, but that didn't stop me from leaning into him, my heart rate picking up. "But what did you hope to find here? You've seen the body; what more do you need?"

"I'm looking for the same thing you are, most likely. You're checking on the people who have keys to the salon, right? But what if it was someone who knew about the hidden key? That could be anybody." I gave him the information like a gift, pretending it wasn't calculated to soften him up.

"I may not be after the same things you are," He smiled and put a hand on my shoulder, softly this time. "But why don't you leave this to me anyway? I'll look around and let you know what I find. That way we both get what we want."

"What do you get out of it?" I asked. But I knew. He wanted me to go away.

"Not to have to worry about you getting yourself shot." His hand slid down my arm until it was lightly circled around my wrist. "That's what I get. I'm much more efficient when I'm not protecting civilians as a by-product of my work."

Bingo. I gently pulled my arm away. The physical contact was distracting me, as it was meant to, no doubt.

"So this is *go away Bree, make my life easy and I'll throw you a bone*, right? Quid pro quo." I kept my voice light, amused not angry that he thought I'd walk away from my responsibility.

"Yep. That's what this is." He was totally relaxed, rocked back on his heels, smiling at me. Except I could see his jaw flex.

"Okay," I said. "I'm outta here. But you'd better hold up your side of the bargain, Hamm—Ham*becker*, or all bets are off." I was still smiling, the non-threatening girl reporter with fluff for brains.

"Absolutely. When I have bones to throw, you'll be the first dog to get them. Stay safe." He turned and trotted away from me, back to the farmhouse and whatever else might be hiding there.

I watched him move effortlessly across the field for a minute, then smiled and made my way back to my truck. Two could play at this game. While Hambecker was tied up here, I'd go somewhere he wasn't. Starting with James Fisk.

I found Jim in his office in Hanover. I'd taken Annie home, changed into business attire and brushed on a little mascara. I figured if I was going to act like a real reporter it couldn't hurt to at least look the part. Before leaving home I slathered Meg's homemade blackberry jam on toast and dropped some on my skirt. I rubbed it with a damp dishrag, and I was pretty sure I'd gotten it all out.

Jim was picking up the phone when his assistant stepped into his office to tell him I was waiting. I know this because I was one step behind her, instead of waiting near her desk as would be customary. I hadn't waited when I dated Jim, and I wasn't going to start now.

His glance slid past her and landed on me, and the furrow in his forehead vanished.

"I've got this, Mary, thanks. Bree, this is unexpected." He smiled and gestured to the chairs facing his desk.

I settled into the deep brown leather and ran my hand over the brass upholstery tacks.

"Very manly chairs," I said. "Are they new?"

"Yeah. I got them when you were in California last fall."

He relaxed into his chair and propped his shoes on the desk. There was gum on the leather sole of his left shoe. I considered telling him, but figured being the bearer of bad news wasn't to my best advantage.

"I didn't know you owned Claire's building," I said. "Have you always?"

"Is that why you're here? To ask about the salon?" The faint edge of anger came through, even though I knew he was trying to hide it.

"No, I came here to say I've reconsidered your offer to take me to Loudon. I only asked about the salon because it popped into my head." I shrugged. "I'm impulsive like that."

"I remember that about you." A half-smile hovered on his lips. "You changed your mind about the races? You do know this is a date, right? We're clear on that?"

"Yes, I know it's a date. I'm impulsive, not stupid."

"Forgive me if I'm a little skeptical. You were pretty adamant about not wanting to go with me. What changed?"

"You surprised me is all. I needed some time to think about it." *And I didn't know you owned the building where I found a dead body.* "Meg encouraged me to reconsider."

"I guess I should write Meg a thank-you note." He put his hands behind his head and relaxed deeper into his chair. Any guilt I was feeling for lying to him disappeared. Smug, self-satisfied bastard.

"Anyway, it'd be fun to go to the races with you again. I haven't been to Loudon since the last time we went together." That was a lie too, I realized. I'd been to the motorcycle races with another friend before I'd headed out to California. *In for a penny, in for a pound.* I smiled at Jim, hoping the fact I hadn't forgiven him wasn't written all over my face. Maybe *forgiven* wasn't the right word. You don't forgive a snake for being a snake, do you? You just recognize them for what they are, and then give them a wide berth.

"Good." He dropped his feet to the floor and leaned forward. "I'll pick you up at the farm around seven Sunday morning." He reached for his phone.

"Wait. Can I talk about the body at Planet Hair? I mean, is your firm involved? I was kind of wondering what the ramifications are for Claire, and when she might get back in her shop." God was going to strike me down for lying. My only consolation was Jim would probably get taken out by the lightning bolt with me.

"We aren't currently... involved, but it's never wise to discuss a current investigation. So no, I won't talk about it with you."

"You aren't willing to speculate?" I was pushing it now, and I knew it. But I wanted to sees his reaction.

"Give me a break, Bree. I'm a lawyer and I own the building where the body was found. No, I'm not going to speculate about it." He reached for the phone again, but he had his eyes on me, questioning.

I gave in. After all, I'd have all day Sunday to subtly grill him. I stood up and shot him my warmest smile. "See you Sunday then."

He was punching numbers on the phone before I was out the door.

I grabbed a veggie sub and ate it in my truck on the way back to South Royalton, oozing olives and shredded lettuce onto my skirt. In the forty minutes it took to get back to South Royalton I'd compiled a whole laundry list of things to investigate, along with a shopping list so I could make my own sandwiches. I hadn't really been an investigative reporter up to this point. Stuff happened, people talked about it and I put it in the paper. Sure, I checked facts and asked questions, but the entire issue was usually right there in front of me. This was different.

Should I go back to school? It was an investment in my future, but I didn't really have the money. How likely was it that I'd see another case like this? Normally, I'd say there was no chance at all, but the three bodies I'd been involved with in the past year indicated I could be wrong. Dead wrong.

I laughed at my own humor, because that's how lame I am.

I thought I was on my way back to the office when the truck developed a mind of its own and turned up the road to Jim's house. Before I knew it I was parked outside his log-built home with my heart pounding. He was at work, the chance that I'd get caught was low, but it still felt wrong. *That's because it is wrong, Bree. B and E can get you jail time.* I didn't even know what I was looking for, a pack of diapers? If not diapers, maybe I'd know it when I saw it.

I almost drove away, but then I remembered Meg's face when Tiny's Trailers called to yank their ad. This was the story that could save us; I knew it in my veggie-filled gut. And just maybe, if I got this right, Meg would pull herself into the twenty-first century and put it online. I made a mental note to look into online newspapers and opened the truck door.

My feet hit the gravel and I was on the front porch trying the door before I could stop myself. Locked.

Locked? Jim never locked his doors. Nobody I knew ever locked their doors. I walked around to the deck and climbed the stairs. The slider into the kitchen was unlocked. He was locking the front door and not the back? Go figure.

I stepped in and slid the door closed behind me. It was quiet and familiar. It had been almost a year since I'd sat at the counter while Jim broke my heart, but the memory was clear and nothing about the place had really changed. There were no fresher memories to dull the emotion.

What the hell was I doing here? I focused on the task at hand and walked through the house room by room looking for... well, looking for *anything*. Some evidence that Jim was involved in the murder. Duckie diapers in a single man's home would have been an excellent clue. But there wasn't anything.

I stepped into his bedroom. There were memories here, too, and not much else. I even riffled through his closet. On the way back down the hall I pulled open the coat closet to take a quick look, mostly out of indecent curiosity. The fact that I'd taken a stupid risk for nothing was just sinking in, when there in the middle of his London Fog raincoat and Burberry overcoat was pair of rumbled and dirty suit pants on a hanger. My heart kicked up and my palms started to sweat. I struggled to remember the suit coat the dead man had been wearing. His pants had been a pin stripe, and I remembered the jacket had been ill-fitting. A grey plaid?

I was pretty sure these ugly pants matched the dead guy's jacket. I checked the size in the waistband. Thirty-six by thirty. Definitely not Jim's, which didn't surprise me; Jim didn't wear ugly clothes. But still, what the hell were they doing in Jim's closet if they weren't Jim's?

I used my phone to take a picture and then high-tailed it out the kitchen door, making sure it was all the way closed and that I hadn't left any sign of myself in the house. I jumped in the truck and got high and away from the area before I allowed myself to think. When I did start to think my mind wouldn't shut up. It raced from one thing to another. Should I call the cops? What about the date on Sunday? Would it be suspicious if I cancelled that? Or maybe I should go on the date so the cops could search his house. I'd be safe at Loudon; I just wouldn't invite him in to my place for drinks afterward.

Shit. What about Hambecker? He was going to be raging mad if he found out I'd searched Jim's house. Well too bad. He wasn't going to find out anyway. If I told anyone it would be Tom Maverick.

My brain was racing and instead of going straight back to the office I took a detour over to the Bethel Barracks. The desk clerk buzzed me through the inner door and I tried to track down Tom in his office, but he couldn't be found. I noticed Steve Leftsky was in the bull pen eating a sandwich while tapping on his computer with one hand. I snagged a rolling chair from a table on the other side of the room and rolled myself over to his desk, grabbing a couple of chips off his napkin. He was looking at me, mouth full, eyebrows up.

"Multitasking?" I asked.

He chewed and swallowed and took a drink of the soda on his desk before he tried to speak. I appreciated him not spewing his sandwich all over me.

"What's up?"

"Ever consider taking smaller bites?" I asked.

"I'm hungry. Haven't eaten all day. Why don't you talk and I'll eat?" He took another bite that looked as though it might choke a horse.

"Does Shirl know you eat like that? It's disgusting."

"Give me a break, I'm hungry. Either talk or get out, I've got work to do."

"Hypothetically, if I happened to see something I thought might be evidence in a crime while I was at someone's house, would that be admissible evidence?"

He frowned and swallowed his bite.

"I thought you were doing the talking, and I was doing the eating," Steve said. He wiped his mouth. "Depends. Were you invited in? Wait!" He held up his hand. "This *is* hypothetical, right? We aren't talking about actual evidence in an actual house are we?"

I wrinkled my nose.

"Hell, Bree. You're going to get us both into trouble, aren't you? Jeez, I should have run when I heard you were in the building."

"But what if I was invited in? Then it would be good. Right? Then I could tell you about it?"

"I do not want you getting yourself invited into a potential murderer's house. I also do not approve of unauthorized entry into anyone's home. You start breaking the law, Bree, Tom will not be able to protect you. You understand that, don't you?"

"Yes. I understand." I also knew he'd get himself fired before he'd see me in jail. I couldn't do that to him or Meg. I'd have to be sneakier.

"Whose home are you hypothetically planning on entering illegally? Off the record."

"James Fisk." I held my breath.

"You're kidding me? You're accusing *Fisk* of murder? Effing *dot-the-I-and-cross-the-T* Fisk? He's never even had a speeding ticket. No way. No effing way. Out!"

He pointed at the door and I didn't exactly run out the door, but I didn't saunter either. I waved at the desk sergeant on the way past, very carefully backed my truck out, and slowly pulled onto route 107. Because it wouldn't be wise to give anyone a reason to arrest me.

Then it hit me that I might have been dating a murderer. I started to laugh and clamped my hand over my mouth. This was no time to get hysterical. I had a story to get. I needed to keep my eye on the prize.

I pulled into the Shell station for an ice cream sandwich and bottle of chocolate milk to calm my nerves.

Lori's kids wore diapers and she had a key to the shop, so I pretty much had to make the trip over the hill to see her. I drove through Sharon with a package of M&Ms in my lap, and orange soda in my cup holder. I took Route 132 over into Strafford, then turned left up over the hill into Thetford. I could have taken the freeway, but that's the long way around. And probably not any faster, even though it is a freeway. The afternoon sun filtered through the trees over-arching the roads, and the air blowing in through my open windows was cool and silky on my skin. Tomorrow it might be hot and sticky, but for now it was perfect. I relaxed and took it slow, enjoying the overgrown beauty that stole over Vermont in the summer. Where warm places like California are dry and brown in the summer, Vermont is lush and green. Of course, that's because it rains all the time, but you can't have everything.

Lori's home was a white clapboard cape on the outskirts of town. It sat back from the main road and I turned onto a dirt drive that wound between stone walls and birch trees for maybe an eighth of a mile before I reached the house. Lori was out front, sitting beside a baby on a blanket while a tiny blond girl tried to ride a large black dog. The dog ignored the toddler's attempt to get on his back until she grabbed his tail at which point he collapsed on the ground with the tiny blond on top of him.

I parked the truck near the house and walked over to the foursome. The dog raised his head, barked once, loudly enough to make me jump and then set his head back down on the ground and let the toddler pull his ears.

"Good dog," I said. "Did you train him to lie down when his tail gets yanked on?" I held out my hand. "I'm Bree MacGowan; I'm a friend of Claire P—"

"I know you. Claire talks about the crazy stuff you get up to. She said you might be over to see me." She reached up and shook my hand.

"Do you mind if we talk a bit?" I felt a little guilty about wanting to talk murder in front of children, but I doubted Lori got much time alone.

"Sit down." She patted the blanket. "I could use some adult company for a change. It's nothing but babies twenty-four seven until my husband gets back from Afghanistan." She looked over at me. "Murder in Planet Hair, huh? How weird is that?"

"Well not *in* the salon exactly. The police say the body was dumped after the fact." Lying was getting too easy, but I didn't want to have to explain my assumptions due of lack of facts.

"Strange place to leave a body. Oh jeez, the baby stinks!" She grabbed her baby by the leg and pulled her gently over. She stuck her hand in a big pink plastic tote and pulled out a cloth diaper and cover, and my suspicions of her innocence were fortified. Lori didn't use disposable diapers. "Ew. I don't care if she is mine; she stinks worse than any baby I've ever seen. Must take after her dad." She grinned at me.

"You use cloth diapers? Aren't they a pain?" I asked.

"I won't use disposable diapers. I just don't feel right about putting those chemicals on my baby's skin. My mom is paying for the diaper service." She fastened on a diaper cover and pulled a pair of tiny blue jeans up over the diaper. The soiled diaper went into in plastic bag. "It works out fine."

"What did you think when you heard there was a dead body in the salon?" I asked her. "Were you surprised?" I waited while she disengaged the toddler's fist from the dog's tail. The dog licked her face and then the baby's. The baby squealed happily and grabbed the dog's ears. The dog lowered his head patiently while Lori removed the tiny fingers from his ear.

"Truthfully, I'm not that shocked." Lori said. "I've heard that Ronnie Hart's brother is mixed up with some pretty rough people."

"Do you know who?" I hadn't even known Ronnie had a brother.

"I probably shouldn't say this, but my brother told my husband that he has a connection to the mob. People like that, who knows why they do what they do." She captured the baby's hands before he could latch onto the dog again.

"The mob?" My heart pumped harder. "New

York?"

"New York. Come here, pumpkin." She picked the baby up and let him balance his weight on his feet for a moment.

"But why dump a body in Planet Hair?" I asked.

Lori shrugged. "Because his sister has a key? Why does anyone do anything? I mean really, if you're going to kill someone, then anything you do after that has got to be the result of an addled brain, don't you think? How could you kill someone and not be addled?"

She blew kisses onto his little neck and rolled back, lifting him into the air, making airplane noises. Her little girl wasted no time straddling her stomach and when Lori rolled back up she had both of them on her lap.

"I never thought of it that way," I said. "I always assume people have good reasons for doing what they do. It may not seem reasonable to me, but to them it's the only thing to be done. How does your brother know Ronnie's brother?"

"My brother was in prison for a while. I guess you hear all sorts of things in there."

It seemed rude to ask what he was in jail for, although I was dying to know. We talked a while longer about things unrelated to the murder before I drove back across the hill, my mind in overdrive.

Chapter Five

On the way home I considered my list of suspects. Jim, Ronnie and Lori. Not a huge list, and none of them seemed a likely murderer. I didn't think either Ronnie or Lori was strong enough to drag a body up the stairs into the salon. Jim probably had plenty of easier options for disposing of a dead body. Dumping the body at Planet Hair stank of desperation and hurry. But even then. Why not the river?

It was hard for me to keep my feelings from clouding the facts. I'd never written an article when it was more important to keep emotion out of it. I didn't want to think that Claire would hire a murderer to clean her shop. I trusted her instincts, but the facts might not justify my trust. Or maybe it wasn't Ronnie, maybe it was someone who knew where she kept the key. Ronnie might not even know if someone had taken the key. I didn't know. I had to stick to the facts, damn it anyway.

Lori? I wanted to say no. I just couldn't see it. She'd never put those babies at risk. They could be mother *and* fatherless if daddy was in Afghanistan and Mommy was in the clink. But still, not fact. I hadn't really been able to rule anyone out, only that if guilt and innocence rested on easy access to disposable ducky diapers, then Lori was out of the picture.

Then it occurred to me, Claire was a suspect too, which gave me a stomach ache. An unlikely suspect, but she had access to the shop if not a handy supply of diapers. What would it take for Claire to kill someone? I didn't know. She'd be demented to dump a dead body in her own shop, though.

Instead of turning right on Route 14 I drove over the bridge into South Royalton and on to Meg's house. I found Claire still in the kitchen snipping away at a tiny blond girl. The girl's mother was hovering, getting in Claire's way and pointing out all the stray hairs that Claire hadn't gotten to yet but the mother felt she'd missed. Claire kept a tight smile on her face and her voice was pleasant, but I thought that deep inside she probably wanted to pop the mother one.

I know I did.

"I have got to get out of here," Claire said after the woman closed the door behind them. "I love that Meg is lending me her kitchen, but I need my stuff. And it doesn't hurt that there are two bars within walking distance of my shop. I need a beer."

"Did she at least leave you a big tip?"

Claire snorted.

"One dollar over the cost of the cut. And I think she would have asked for the change back if she'd dared. I've got to call Tom and see if I can get my space back." She zipped around gathering up the tools of her trade. "Then I have to see if Ronnie will clean it, or if I have to get some kind of crime scene professionals. Thank God there's no blood." She hiked her bag onto her shoulder. "Are you waiting for Meg? Or did you need me for something? Your cut looks good."

"Yeah, great job. I was wondering how you felt about Ronnie as a suspect? Could she commit murder?"

"I think anyone can kill in the right circumstances, but Ronnie? I don't think so. She's really just a child, emotionally and mentally. But other than her? If someone was going to kill Meg and you had the chance to stop that from happening, what would you do?"

"Good point. I just can't get my head around someone bringing a dead person to Planet Hair. Why would anyone do that? If I had a dead body I'd dump it in the woods or the river, I wouldn't drag it into Planet Hair."

"Didn't Tom tell you? They dug a bullet out of the wall. He *was* killed at the salon." Claire was packing up her tools as we talked.

"But there wasn't any blood!" I'd been there. Not a drop of blood anywhere. And Tom was officially on my shit list.

"I know. Weird huh? And the door to the thrift shop next door was jimmied open. But they can't tell if anything was taken." She slung her bag over her shoulder and looked at me expectantly. She wanted to go.

"Someone killed a man at Planet Hair at eleven o'clock at night, cleaned up the mess, re-dressed the guy in clean clothes, *after* taping diapers to him and left. Taking all the bloody rags and clothes with them. That's just as bizarre at killing him elsewhere and dumping him there." I was confused. I remembered the saying about the simplest solution usually being right, but what if there wasn't a simple solution?

"I know. Right? It doesn't make any sense. I'll see you later, I need to get home." She was moving toward the door.

"Sure," I said. "Leave me here in my confusion."

"Hang out for a while, I'm sure Meg will show up and then you can be confused together."

She laughed and headed out. I followed after; it

was time to feed the animals and I wanted to know
what Hambecker had learned.

"Think of the devil," I said as I walked up the steps
to my kitchen porch. Hambecker was leaning against
the door, wearing jeans and a nearly skin-tight black T-
shirt. Leaning on the door was an improvement
considering in the past he'd just walked right on in.
Really it had only been twice, once I'd been asleep and
the other time I hadn't been here at all, but still I was
kind of surprised he wasn't already in the kitchen
drinking a beer.

"Do you know you've got a skunk hanging
around?" he asked. "I would have disposed of it for
you, but I thought it might be against your principles, so
I left it alone."

"That's Stripes! He's Diesel's best friend. You kill
Stripes and you're a dead man." It hadn't occurred to
me that someone would kill him thinking they were
doing me a favor. I took a few deep breaths in an
attempt to slow my heart rate.

"Who's Diesel? A demented raccoon?" Hambecker
raised one eyebrow.

"No, smart ass, he's my boxer." I walked past him
and pushed the door open. I stood still for a minute
while the dogs surged around us, sniffing at Hambecker
before running into the yard. I dropped my bag on a
chair and opened the fridge. "Thirsty?"

"Sure." He slid out a chair and sat at the kitchen

table facing the door.

I handed him a bottle of Old Excuses – a local beer from the Freight House - and sat at the end of the table so I could be facing the door too. Not that I was expecting anybody, I just didn't want to be the fool who sat with her back to the door.

"Who are we waiting for?" I asked, nodding toward the door.

"Nobody that I know of."

"Why are we sitting here watching the door?"

"Force of habit," he said. "It doesn't hurt to be prepared."

"Don't you ever just relax? What's going to happen up here on the hill? I supposed a rabid porcupine might get the door open and attack us."

"It's not porcupines I'm worried about. You want to tell me why you still don't bother to lock your doors? It's like I never abducted you."

"Would a locked door have stopped you?"

"Nope."

"Would it stop anyone who was determined to get in?"

"Nope."

"I rest my case."

"I can't argue with that." He set his bottle on the table. He seemed relaxed, but that muscle in his jaw flexed. Now that I knew where it was I could tell when he wasn't as relaxed as he pretended to be. I liked to think that it gave me an edge.

"Wouldn't matter if you did. Now tell me what you found at Ronnie Hart's place."

His face was partially turned away from me. *Hiding something*, I thought.

"Not much. No signs of unusual activity. I found

some diapers under the tractor in her shed. They were soaking up oil dripping from her tractor. But with only that to go on I wouldn't say there's much reason to investigate further."

"What about the burn spot in the back of the shed? That looked pretty fresh."

"Come on, Bree. Three-quarters of the people in this state have a burn pile on their property. I'll bet I'd find one behind your barn if I looked."

This was true. I did have a burn pile. I didn't burn my garbage the way some people did, but I did burn scrub and old hay sometimes. Fallen branches and stuff like that. Then I put the ash in my compost pile.

Hammie leaned into me. "Listen, I'm going to tell you something that I probably shouldn't, but I want you to know the kind of people we are dealing with here. The guy you found is Albin Shvakova, a professional killer from Eastern Europe."

"Are you kidding me? A Russian hitman ended up dead at Planet Hair?"

"Bulgarian. He was in the country illegally, likely for a hit. I'm speculating here, but in all likelihood someone smuggled him across the border, either through the Akwesasne Mohawk reservation in New York—a lot traffic comes through there—or across the border here in Vermont."

"I heard there was a problem with human trafficking." I hadn't, however, considered what kinds of people were being smuggled across the border. It made Vermont seem a little less safe; and I didn't like that.

"Do you have any idea what kind of people would risk smuggling an assassin across the American border?" He tapped his bottle gently on the edge of the table.

"Dangerous people?" I felt like saying 'well duh' but I figured as long as he was feeding me information I was going to play along like a nice girl.

"Beyond dangerous. We think he has connections to the mob in New York and Paris. Stay out of this. Stay away from Ronnie Hart. I don't do my best work when I'm trying to keep you alive, so I'm asking you nicely. Let me do my job. If you do that I promise I'll give you as much information as I can. That's the deal. You stay safe and I'll give you what you need to write your article."

I wanted to say yes to him. I really did. But when it came down to it, I couldn't give up like that. I needed to do my own work. Find out the answers he might not be willing to feed me.

I said, "No."

"What?" He looked at me through narrowed eyes.

"I can't promise that. I appreciate you are willing to feed me information, but what if I've got questions you can't answer? What if you can't tell me what I need to know? Your boss or whoever might object. I can't tell you I won't go looking for answers if that happens. Someone killed a hitman and left him in my friend's salon. My community is impacted by this. My home town." I was starting to sound like some kind of activist. Jeez, could I get any cornier?

"Crap," he said. "I knew you were going to say that." He turned and looked me full in the face. "I'm going to have to handcuff you to something again, aren't I?"

"You wouldn't dare." I pushed my chair back and went to the door and opened it. The dogs surged back in. "You don't mind if I let the dogs in do you?" Not that I cared if he minded. If Hambecker got it into his head to handcuff me to something I was going to need my dogs. If nothing else they could trip him up while I ran for the truck.

"I'm not planning on doing it now, if that's what you're worried about." He reached out and rubbed Ranger on the top of his head and behind his ears. "I was thinking of what might happen in the future, and what I might have to do about it. That's all."

"Ranger, come here." The wolfhound came and sat at my feet leaning against my leg so that I had to take a step back and lean against the counter to keep from falling over. "I *will* endeavor not to get in the way of your job as official federal agent. But if you try and handcuff me to something just because I'm doing my job as investigative reporter, I will bring the wrath of the MacGowans down upon your head. I have two rather burly brothers and a whole slew of friends who get agitated when guys mess with me."

My brothers are not exactly the kind of guys you'd normally call *burly*. They're biggish and pretty strong and will defend me if they have to. But they'd rather not, really. They appreciate the fact that most of the time I'm pretty good at taking care of myself. They did teach me how to shoot, and to go for the eyes and the gonads under duress, and I think they felt that was the extent of their brotherly duties. They knew I occasionally threatened guys with them and they were fine with that as long as I didn't actually call on them to defend my honor.

"You think I'd let your brothers stop me?" He was amused and I could tell he was trying not to smile. "Honey, bring it on. I'd be happy to handcuff you to your brothers. That would save me from having to stick around."

"Oh, please," I said, rolling my eyes. He was playing Hambecker the Neanderthal.

Beagle Annie collapsed at his feet, rolling over to show him her belly. He rubbed the toe of his boot gently across her ribs before spearing me with his eyes.

"If I understand my source correctly, you failed to mention that you'd been doing some snooping around of your own, MacGowan. Find anything?" His tone was light and there wasn't a sign of anger in his face, but I felt like I was facing The High Court of South Royalton.

"I didn't tell you because I didn't find a dang thing. Total waste of time. But I did save you the trouble." I breathed slowly, willing my heart to slow. Why did he make me so damn nervous?

"Really? Nothing?"

I opened my eyes wide and nodded my head like one of those bobble head dogs. But that only caused Hambecker to narrow his eyes at me.

"Funny, Steve Leftsky seemed to think you might have come across something unusual. I must have misheard him." He looked me square in the eye and my stomach squirmed. "Did I mishear him, Bree? Or are you keeping something from me?" He tapped his finger on the arm table. "Spill."

I contemplated lying, running for the door or hurdling out the window but he was going to catch me sooner or later so I caved.

"There isn't anything to tell. I found a pair of pants that I thought matched the suit jacket the dead guy was wearing. Steve told me I was nuts when I told him whose closet I found them in. He threw me out of his office. Didn't exactly make me want to tell anyone else." Especially not Hambecker.

"Where?" He had me fixed with his eyes.

"A closet."

"Was it a closet you were invited to look into?" He was feigning patience.

"No. But it was a closet I'd visited in the past." And I would break him before he broke me.

"I take it that would be Jim Fisk's closet?" The front legs of the chair clunked to the ground as Hambecker sat forward. Beagle Annie jumped up and gave him a dirty look. "Easy there, girl," he said quietly and reached down to rub her head.

"Yeah. So?" I said.

"You were in his home uninvited?" He was unblinking.

"You already know that." I was staring back. Two could play at this game.

"Listen carefully. I want you to stay the hell out of Jim Fisk's house. This is not a game, Bree."

"I know it's not a game, damn it. The future of the paper could be riding on this story. I'm not sitting around waiting for some guy to throw me a bone." I narrowed my eyes.

"Stay away from Jim." I imagined I saw his jaw flex again but it could have been a trick of the clouds blocking the sun from the windows for a moment.

"I can't. I have plans to see him." I moved just a little farther from the table.

"You made a plan to see Jim?" He looked down at the floor and I was finally able to blink.

"Sure. I'm going to the races with him Sunday."

"You have a date with James Fisk?" I didn't imagine the jaw clench this time. He was going to need dental work if he kept this up. "Great. Perfect."

"You know me, I like to plan ahead." I turned my back to him and pretended to straighten the papers on the counter. After three excruciating minutes, during which he didn't take the hint, I turned back around.

"You're still here? I thought you'd be out the door and off to the next black op, or whatever you call what you do." I gestured to the door.

"I'm not leaving until I'm sure you will be careful and play by the rules. I won't be able to help you if you get yourself arrested, and I can't spend all my time watching you to make sure you don't get yourself into a situation you can't get out of." He was rubbing Beagle Annie with his foot again, not looking at me.

"Excuse me? Play by the rules? This is from the guy who injected me with drugs and dragged me across country." The double standard was absurd.

Hambecker had the bad judgment to grin at that. "Yeah, I enjoyed that. I don't get to use my training as much as I'd like."

"Your training!" I snorted. "You trained to abduct women from their beds?"

"No, I trained to abduct fascist dictators from their beds. Of course, dictators are easier to handle, but I was up to the challenge." He stood up and took a step toward me.

I sucked in a couple of really big breaths and counted to ten in my head. I was a little bit proud that he found me a pain in the ass to control.

"And another thing," I said. "I'm perfectly capable of taking care of myself – as you well know." I wasn't entirely successful at keeping the glee out of my voice. He may have been able to abduct me with the help of a knockout drug, but he hadn't been able to keep me contained.

"Don't get cocky," he said.

"I'm not the one that got too cocky," I said. "I'm the one that escaped your clutches. And don't worry. I don't plan on being caught sleeping again. I've been taking precautions since you've been back in town." My precautions were to lock the bedroom door, keep the dogs in my room with me at night and hang bells on the door handle. The dogs, unfortunately, were bribable and the lock was pickable, so I was counting on the bells waking me up before anyone got in the door. The fact that I couldn't sleep in the summer unless my window was open was a problem, but I could hang bells in front of it too. I pulled a Post It from the drawer under the counter and wrote "buy more bells."

"Is that a challenge?" he asked. "Because it sounds like a challenge. I can't afford to back down from challenges. My reputation is hanging by a string here."

"Your reputation?" I slid one step away from him, along the counter top. Beagle Annie noticed my movement and came to stand between Hambecker and me. I heard the low grumble of her warning growl, but I don't think he did.

"Yeah, that's what happens when I hang out around you. Very hard on the rep, and you wouldn't believe the ribbing I've been taking. Don't make any challenges you don't want me to take. I'm thinking snatching you from under the watchful eye of Tom Maverick would go a long way toward restoring the faith." He took another step forward, his eyes on mine again.

Oh, brother.

"Okay then, not a challenge, just a statement." I waved him away. "See you later. I've got work to do."

"Yeah, me too."

He was gone before I realized I was holding my breath. Damn. I sucked in air and watched his SUV drive away throwing a rooster tail of dust in its wake. I'd gotten one thing from our little tussle. He wanted me to stay out of Ronnie Hart's house.

Which meant there was something there to see.

Chapter Six

An hour later, I was dressed in black jeans, bright blue girl-cut tee, black leather jacket, motorcycle boots, and I had my gloves and helmet in my hand. One way to keep myself from drinking too much free beer was to ride my motorcycle. It was always safety first with my dad, and it stuck.

The phone rang as I was about to step out the door. I debated answering for a moment, then dropped my helmet and gloves on the table and picked up the phone.

Silence.

"I'm about to hang up the phone so if you want to talk to me you'd better speak."

I thought I heard faint breathing.

"Okay then." I hung up the phone.

It hadn't rained in ages so the roads were dry. I made good time down the hill, felt the cool rush of air as I crossed the river and pulled the bike up onto its center stand on the sidewalk in front of the insurance agency. Parking would be at a premium tonight.

The bar was already packed when I walked in. Grant stood in a circle of people near the bar, but he noticed and shot me the thumbs-up. I sent him a smile and returned the thumbs-up, searching for a place where I wouldn't be jostled too much.

Claire flagged me down and I joined her at a pub table in front of the window. The waitress plunked a couple of pints on the table and took our food order. There were a couple of empties, so I bussed the table to give us more room and sat down, resting my heels on the rung of the stool.

"Glad you're here," Claire started but then glanced behind me and smiled.

I felt a hand on my shoulder and looked up to see Grant standing behind me, his surfer hair curling up from his head like a slightly younger, curly-haired Channing Tatum. He still had the thin wiry body of a young athlete with none of the bulk men sometimes develop as they mature. He was probably five or six years behind me in school, so I didn't know him well. But everyone in town knew of him. He was like the Law School, one of our claims to fame.

"Doing all right, ladies?" he asked. "Drink as much as you like, it all on me tonight – and it doesn't have to be beer. If you'd rather a mixed drink, go for it. Let me know if any of these yahoos bother you, I'll take care of it. Can't have the hometown girls getting hassled."

Having done his social duty Grant melted back into the crowd. Claire and I called our thanks after him, and Claire sighed.

"When did we get too old for guys like that?" she asked as we watched Grant sling his arm around a woman barely out of high school. But then he slung his other arm around a woman almost old enough to be my mother and planted a kiss on her.

"I don't know," I said. "Maybe were not too old. He's an equal-opportunity... what's the word? I don't want to say *womanizer*. I don't think it's that."

"Flirt?" Claire asked.

"Yeah, an equal-opportunity flirt." Whatever we labeled him, he was lifting the atmosphere in the bar.

Even I was relaxed and having a good time until a hand dropped on the back of my neck and I nearly jumped out of my skin.

"Hambecker," I said when I looked to see who had disturbed my bliss. "I didn't know you hung out with the locals."

"Occasionally. I saw your bike outside. You're not drinking and riding." It wasn't a question, but I could tell he was puzzled.

"One beer," I motioned to my glass, "and soda. You can stop worrying."

"I wasn't worried. Just surprised." He snagged a stool from the next table and sat down with us. "What's the occasion? This place isn't usually packed like this."

"Grant Fraser, that's him over there. The guy with his arm around the dark haired girl." I said.

"The surfer dude," Claire added.

"The tall guy," Hambecker said.

"Yeah, the tall guy. He's a Formula 1 racer. Grew up here. Whenever he wins big he flies back to town and it's free drinks and racing stories until the bar closes. See, he's telling one now."

Grant's free hand was driving an imaginary car, while his mouth was going a mile a minute. I couldn't hear what he was saying, but it had to be good because the crowd around him roared. He grinned, released the brunette and took a swig from a glass on the bar. I'd watched the bartender pour it. He was drinking soda water.

"You want to meet him? I'll introduce you," I said.

Grant was charming. He looked slightly taken aback at Hambecker's bulk, but he rallied. "Bree, got yourself a body guard?" He stuck out his hand and the ensuing handshake was some moronic male test of strength, but they were both grinning. When they broke the grip Grant maneuvered himself so that he stood between Hambecker and me and threw his arm around my shoulder. He planted a kiss on my cheek and I watched to see if Hambecker would object.

But Hambecker launched into a discussion of some other Formula 1 driver they apparently both knew. My eyes glazed over and I wondered if I could slip out from under Grant's arm and go sit down. But when I went to disengage myself Grant tightened his hold and I drifted, not paying attention to the shop talk.

I felt Grant's arm loosen about the time he said, "Nice meeting you, man. Let me know if you want to come to the races and I'll get you a hot pass."

I want a hot pass.

"Thanks, Grant, I'll do that," Hambecker said, and he draped his arm across my shoulder during the pass off. He led me back to the table where Claire was chatting with one of Grant's pit crew. My drink had disappeared and I was about to go up to the bar for another when Hambecker plunked a beer in front of me.

"Thanks," I said, "but I can't. I already had a beer."

"That had to be a couple of hours ago, you could probably have another." He tipped back his mug and drank.

"One's my limit when riding, thanks."

"You can ride home with me." He leaned against the window watching me. He had that danged half-smile on his face again and alarm bells were going off in my head. *There be monsters here.*

Only it was more like *there be heartbreak here.*

"You're going the wrong direction." I smiled and kicked myself down off the stool. "Anyhow, it's time for me to go home. I forgot to feed Stripes before I left. Wouldn't want the resident skunk getting mad, would I?"

"Guess not." He looked sorry I was leaving. Huh. I was kind of happy about that.

The little bit of information that Hambecker had thrown my way the day before got me thinking about connections. Ronnie's brother was connected to the mob in New York City. Ledroit came from New York looking for a man named Puccini. A Bulgarian assassin was found dead in the Planet Hair, which Ronnie cleaned. Someone dangerous and powerful had smuggled the assassin over the border. The mob was dangerous and powerful and could be from New York. A coincidence? Maybe, but I didn't think so.

Instead of parking in the lay-by the next morning, I pulled onto a dirt track that the farmer used to pull his tractor into the orchard. The shrubs along the edge of the road were overgrown and all I had to do was park behind them and my truck was invisible. I tossed the paper plate from the sticky bun I'd picked up at the café on the seat, got out and followed the same path out through the field, but this time I headed straight for the house. I'd taken a good look at the yard when I'd driven by and I knew from my earlier experience that the shed was too full of junk to hold a vehicle.

I walked straight up to the door and knocked loudly before I tried the handle. I pressed my ear to the door and listened intently for a couple of minutes, hoping nobody came driving by and wondered what I was doing. As I expected, the door was unlocked and I slid in and shut it behind me. I stood in the quiet kitchen for a moment, contemplating locking the door from the inside. I decided that locking it would be a huge red flag to anyone coming to the door, so I left it.

I stood in the kitchen listening to the silence for several minutes. I heard my heart pounding and a tractor chug by out on the road, but nothing else. I stepped quietly through the kitchen to the living room. The shades were drawn against the summer sun making the room dim and cool. The floor was odd, bare wood, which was pretty normal except it was shiny and new in the middle and dull around the edges. The couch looked old and comfy, draped with a tan slipcover and dotted with throw pillows.

A child's stuffed doll was hanging off the cushion, its arms and hair dangling. I was tempted to pick the doll up and set her properly on the couch, but I stopped myself. *Touch nothing*, I told myself. *Disturb nothing*.

I crept from room to room. Signs of the family were everywhere: toys in the tub, Matchbox car in the hall. Even in the master bedroom, there was a stuffed bear on the bed and tiny fluffy pink slippers on the floor. The second floor housed a couple of unused rooms, a bathroom and a back bedroom which held only a dresser and mattress on the floor. The drawers in the dresser were empty, but a rumpled sheet and blanket were on the bed, and there was a dent in the pillow. It felt like someone was sleeping there but not inhabiting the room.

I started down the stairs debating with myself about searching the basement. The image in my head

CRAZY LITTLE THING CALLED DEAD

was of a damp dirt floor, fieldstone foundation and creepy-crawlies everywhere. There would be either an ancient furnace or a wood stove for heating the house in the winter. Not my idea of a fun place to hang out.

Before I was back on the main floor the crunch of gravel alerted me to a car pulling into the drive. I did a decent imitation of a dog on roller skates for about five seconds before bolting down the remaining stairs, into the kitchen and through the only door I hadn't opened.

I was lucky. The door really did open onto the basement stairs and not a pantry or broom closet. I stood on the top step with my ear pressed against the door forcing myself to take slow, even breaths. My heart was pounding in my ears and my knees were quivering. Fear of discovery had just ratcheted up the stakes. A bunch.

A bang signaled the kitchen door being thrown open and I got ready to bolt down the stairs if I needed to. Then it occurred to me that by the time I'd realized I needed to move it would be too late. I inched down the dark stairs trying to keep to the edges so the stairs wouldn't creak.

It was black at the foot of the stairs. I could hear cupboards being slammed shut in concert with muffled curses. Then the footsteps hurried out onto the porch and the door slammed. Silence blanketed the house again. I put my hand out, searching for the stair rail.

I crept back up the stairs and listened at the door. Quiet. I groped for the door handle, but it wouldn't turn. It was locked from the other side. I thunked my head on the door, but the noise echoed and scared me. Had the door been locked when I came through it? I didn't suppose it mattered how the door got locked, except if Ronnie had realized someone was in the house and the cops were going to show up. I'd have trouble explaining this one to them.

I felt around on the wall until I found a light switch and flicked it on. A single bulb over my head cast uneven light over the stairs. I was here, might as well explore the basement. I crept down the stairs, not entirely convinced I wanted to be in an old farmhouse basement. There'd be spiders, for sure, and probably rodents as well.

I don't know why I was surprised to find that the basement had been renovated. The old flagstone was gone. The foundation and floors were cemented in. One side was an open area with trikes and skates, and a big table covered in crafts. Small windows ran along the top of the sill. Probably too small for me to squeeze through. No places to hide anything really, unless it fit in a small wooden toy box in the corner of the room. I didn't want to see anything that could be hidden there. A couple of small pet dishes sat on the floor on the other side of the toy box.

I reminded myself that the dead body had already been found and trotted over and lifted the lid. I pulled a red velvet cape off the top. Under that was a magician's hat, a very ratty stuffed bear, and a princess dress. I let out my breath. Nothing nefarious here.

I walked back past the stairs, over to the other side of the basement. This side had been divided into three rooms. The first was a doorless and scrupulously clean laundry area. The same little windows ran along two sides and I could see the front lawn and the road beyond that. I was startled to see the hay field I had come through clearly through the north widows. I'd have to remember that if I ever came back here. Of course, it could be seen from the other windows on this side of the house too, so what did it matter? There was a washer, dryer, a big table with stacks of tiny clothes neatly folded and cabinets above the machines. Pretty boring. I did a cursory look through the cabinets, which got me nothing but laundry products, canning jars filled with preserves and various odds and ends. I took a small basket off one shelf, but found only loose change, tiny toys and a watch, obviously pocket pickings.

The next two rooms had doors, which made me a little nervous, but I figured as long as I was there I really should take a look. A soft sound in the play area caught my attention and I considered going back for a second look, but it was probably the cat whose dishes I saw.

The second room held purple and pink sleds, a wagon, gardening tools and a bulkhead door to the outside. A possible escape route when I'd finished my reconnoitering. I looked around at the plant pots, rakes and bags of soil, but if there was anything suspicious here I wasn't seeing it.

The next room was locked. I wondered if that was suspicious but considering small children used the basement as a play area I thought not. Any number of hazardous materials could be found in a basement. A smart mom would lock them up. I felt over the door and looked along the windowsill for the key. I went back to the laundry room and checked the walls for key hooks and the cabinets once again. Nothing. I found a safety pin in the basket of odds and ends, straightened it out and took it to the door, but it wouldn't budge. It wasn't one of those pushbutton knobs they put on bathrooms. It was a real keyhole and I didn't have the skills needed to unlock it.

I considered putting my foot to it, but I wasn't comfortable damaging Ronnie's door, especially as I might make it unlockable and I had no desire to be responsible for a toddler eating rat poison. I went back into the room with the bulkhead door, which wasn't locked—why would it be?—and let myself out. I shut the heavy doors quietly behind me. And this time I jogged out to the road because I had the uncomfortable feeling I was being watched.

Interestingly enough, the black Cadillac Escalade was in my drive when I got home. By the time I'd parked my Toyota, Hambecker was leaning against his passenger door, legs crossed, one hand absently petting Diesel's head, behind them, down the hill a little, I could see Stripes sniffing around the chicken enclosure. Not that I'd admit it to anybody but I was a little nervous about Hambecker being there. There was no way he knew where I'd been, right? But I mentally prepared myself for battle anyway.

"Hey, Trouble," he said as I slid from my truck and shut the door behind me. "What you been up to? I checked for you back at the office, but Meg said she hadn't seen you today."

"I had stuff to do. I do occasionally have to research my stories. What did you need?"

"Just checking up on you, making sure you weren't sticking your nose into places it might get broken."

"You were worried I might get my nose broken? That's a little bizarre, even for you." I'd already told him that I could take care of myself, thank you very much, what more did he want? I hitched my bag over my shoulder. "I appreciate your concern, but as I remember it I did better than you the last time you were keeping an eye on me. Maybe I should be keeping tabs on you."

"Funny," he said, his voice dead serious. "You're a laugh a minute, MacGowan. Fine. Go do your amateur hour investigation thing, just don't come crying to me when people start shooting at you. I'm telling you, Bree, these people don't care you're just a small town reporter trying to get a story. They'll kill you without hesitation if you get in their way. Hell, they'll kill you if they think you might be *considering* getting in their way."

"Don't get your boxers in a bunch. I'm not getting in anyone's way here. I'm just writing about a small town murder for a small town paper. Nobody cares what I'm doing."

Hambecker shook his head and pushed himself off the Escalade. "Why do I always get stuck with the women who insist they can take care of themselves? Just once I'd like to end up with a woman with a sense of self-preservation who wants to stay out of harm's way. Just once. Is that too much to ask?" He headed around to the driver side. "Listen, MacGowan," he said. "Watch your back. These people are deadly."

"What people?" I asked. "What people are deadly? Is it the Italian Mafia?"

He just shook his head at me and got in the truck. Not that I cared. I already had a good idea of who I was dealing with. I turned and walked into the house without looking back, but I didn't hear the SUV reverse out of the drive until after I shut the door behind me. Round one to MacGowan.

The trouble with claiming victory was that I had no idea how to find out who Hambecker thought had killed the guy. I could, and would, write up what I had, but it wasn't much. I grabbed a pad of lined paper and sat at the kitchen table with an orange creamsicle yogurt and a chocolate chip cookie. The yogurt was lunch. The chocolate chip cookie? Inspiration.

I ended up just doodling on the pad while I rubbed Beagle Annie's belly with my foot because it had dawned on me that if I wanted to find out what Hambecker knew, I was going to have to follow him, which wouldn't be easy. As much as I liked to give him a bad time, he was kind of good at his job. It was going to take a lot of ingenuity on my part not to get caught.

I grabbed my phone and dialed Steve. I knew for a fact that Tom wouldn't tell me what I wanted to know. If I caught Steve off guard I might be able to get him to spill. *Might* being the operative word.

"Hey Steve," I said. "Do you know where Richard Hambecker is staying? I need to get in touch with him."

"I'm surprised you don't know, MacGowan. He's staying with Meg and Tom."

I hung up and fumed for a while before I called Meg.

"You're holding out on me," I said. "Hambecker is staying with you."

"Only since yesterday, Bree. I was going to tell you when I saw you. I just haven't seen you since Tom moved Richard in. He was staying at a hotel in White River Junction. That just wasn't right." Meg Maverick, mother to the masses.

"What isn't right is that no one is telling me anything. The silence is deafening here. But can you do me a favor?" Guilt almost always worked on Meg.

She had to say yes. How can you totally keep your best friend out of the loop and then not owe her one?

You can't. Which is how I ended up parked in a lay-by a quarter mile from Meg's house at noon, waiting for a phone call. I was in Beau's masonry truck. He was building walls in Europe and while he hadn't strictly given me permission to drive his vehicle, he didn't normally have a problem with it.

I had bacon on toast sandwich and Beagle Annie to help keep me company. And an extra-large coffee that I'd stirred chocolate syrup into.

My phone chirped and I read the message: *On the move. Coming your way.*

Good. I turned the key and put the truck in gear, ready to follow Hambecker when he passed me. I pulled one of Beau's old ball caps over my eyes in a sort of disguise and slid down in the seat, pretending to be talking on the phone.

Hambecker zipped by without even a second look at me or the truck. I pulled out behind him, keeping him in sight, but hopefully far enough away that I wouldn't show up on his radar. We drove through Sharon and onto the interstate. Fifteen minutes later he surprised me by taking I-91 South. Not that I wasn't ready to follow him, but why south?

"Why is he going south, Annie?" I asked her. She just licked my hand and laid her head in my lap. Beagle Annie didn't care what direction we went, as long as she got to come with me.

An hour later we'd reached Brattleboro at the southern end of Vermont, and he wasn't showing any signs of stopping. I was out of gas.

I pulled off the interstate to fill up Beau's gas-eating behemoth and started for home. There was no way I was going to be able to pick up Richard again. He could be going anywhere. Well, maybe not anywhere. I was pretty sure he wasn't headed to Canada.

I had a lot of time to think on the way back and I pulled off in West Lebanon and drove to the Radio Shack. For fifty bucks I was able to purchase a GPS tracking unit, which I took home and charged.

The next day I played with the GPS tracker to get the hang of it then I dropped it in my bag and took it to work with me.

"Still mad at me?" Meg asked as I came in the door.

I dropped my stuff on the floor behind my desk and turned to her.

"That depends."

"On what?" Meg's eyes started to narrow.

"On whether or not you'll hide something in Hambecker's Escalade for me."

"Are you kidding? No way am I putting anything in Richard's vehicle. Don't tell me what it is. I don't want to know."

"It's a—"

"No! I meant it when I said don't tell me. I do not want to know *anything* about this. Do you understand? The man is a guest in my house and a federal agent. I am not going to jail because my best friend is an idiot."

"I'm only trying to elevate the status of your newspaper, you know. You might at least pretend to be grateful."

Meg snorted. "Oh yeah, I'm grateful. Grateful I

wasn't in Beau's truck with you when you were following *Agent* Hambecker yesterday. Jeez, Bree, what are you thinking?"

"I'm thinking he knows something he's not telling me. I'm thinking I could find out what it is he knows. I'm thinking I'm an investigative reporter."

Meg slammed her palm down on her desk.

"You just kill me, you know that? You slouch around writing the stories that get dropped in your lap, and then, when Hambecker appears you suddenly turn into Jane Mayer. This paper is not going to live or die on what you write. Only—wait—if you were writing your columns from jail, *that* might increase circulation. Never mind, you can do any crazy thing you want. Just don't get yourself killed." Meg shrugged herself into her coat.

"Don't forget you're coming to dinner tonight." She picked up her purse and stomped out of the room.

I didn't take it personally. We'd been friends long enough that I knew she'd come around again before long. She wouldn't, however, put the tracking device in Hambecker's SUV for me. That was clear. And truthfully, if he'd been a guest at my house I probably wouldn't have done it for her. There are rules.

Well, okay, maybe I would, but only if she had a good reason.

The table was already set when I walked into Meg's kitchen. Unfortunately, she wasn't the person I found there; Hambecker was stirring something on the stove. He turned and looked at me. I'd foolishly stopped half way into the kitchen, frozen by the sight of him. I was an idiot. I told myself to relax and came to stand next to the stove. The familiar smell of spaghetti sauce wafted to me, and my stomach growled. Loudly.

"I didn't know you were cooking tonight when Meg asked me to dinner. I've never seen you cook. I thought Moose was the cook between the two of you." I couldn't seem to stop the idiot words from coming out of my mouth.

"Moose is the cook when he's around because he likes to cook more than I do. Gives him something to hide behind. That doesn't mean I can't cook."

I edged toward the living room. "Excuse me a minute. I want to say hi to Meg."

"Sure. Go ahead."

I practically ran up the stairs to Meg and Tom's bedroom. Meg was sitting with her youngest, brushing her hair.

"You might have warned me." I plopped onto the bed next to her, letting my body fall back until I was staring at the ceiling. "I just made a huge ass of myself."

"Language," said Meg, nodding her head toward Gemma whose hair she was now braiding. "What does it matter? You knew he was staying here."

"God, I don't know. Why do I always make such a fool of myself?" I flipped over on my stomach and looked out the window to the river. If I only had a boat I could float away. *Oh stop being so dramatic. He's just guy.*

"I'd think you'd be used to it by now." Meg laughed.

"Hey!" I picked up a pillow and thumped her back with it. "Be nice."

"I thought the point of best friends was you didn't have to be nice."

"Momma, you always tell me I have to be nice to Toby," Gemma said. She looked confused.

"Yes, I do pumpkin, because you and Toby are still little. When you're grown up you can tease your friends and they'll know when you're kidding." Meg snapped a hair tie on the braid. "Come on," she said. "Richard will think we're afraid to eat his food."

"Wait a sec," I said quietly, so Gemma wouldn't hear. "Can you distract Hambecker for a couple of minutes for me? I don't want him to see what I'm doing."

"Bree!" Meg gave me the don't-you-dare look she'd perfected on her kids.

"Come on Meg, just two minutes."

She huffed down the stairs without answering but I knew she'd do it.

When we got to the kitchen with Gemma and Jeremy—who came out of his room and followed us down the stairs—Tom was there. He was running water over lettuce as Hambecker drained the noodles in the second sink. They were laughing, and obviously comfortable with each other. Like they were friends or something.

Huh. When did they become friends?

Meg motioned for me to get out the door. "Richard, come look at this," she said.

And then I was out the door. I trotted over to the Escalade and yanked on the passenger door. Locked. "What's with these people?" I tried the rear passenger side door, the driver's door and the seat behind the driver. All locked. Rear hatch. Locked. "Crap!"

I ran over to my truck and grabbed a roll of black

duct tape from my *unlocked* glove compartment. I skidded back to Hambecker's SUV and crouched down next to the rear wheel. I wrapped the GPS in duct tape and stuck it to the top of the fender inside the wheel well. I tossed the duct tape into the bed of my truck and sauntered back into the house like I hadn't broken into a sweat.

Meg and Hambecker were just walking in from the living room, and if looks could kill, I'd be dead.

Chapter Seven

Meg called the other two kids down and we sat down to a table loaded with food. The usual madhouse followed with plates and bowls being passed across the table in all directions. Gemma up-ended the basket of rolls and several tumbled off the table to be snapped up by the dogs. It was a normal dinner at chez Maverick.

It wasn't until we all had food on our plates and the kids had silenced themselves by filling their mouths that I noticed that Tom had his *I have to do something I don't want to do* face on. He was serious and there was a furrow between his eyebrows.

"You alright?" I asked him between mouthfuls.

He grimaced. "Let's leave it 'till later, Bree. I don't want to ruin dinner."

I glanced at Meg who shrugged and then at Hambecker who steadfastly refused to meet my eyes. "No," I said. "Let's not."

"Come on, Bree. Richard made us an excellent dinner and I don't want to ruin it with shop talk." Tom smiled at me. "Please."

I thought of all the years I'd known him. The way he and my brother JW watched my back. How he'd never turned his back on me, even sided with me against Meg at times. All that history bore down on me and I wanted to play nice, I really did. But I couldn't back down.

I put down my fork and looked down at my plate.

"No."

"No, what?" Meg asked.

"No, I'm not going to stop investigating this case."

"Damn it," Tom cursed under his breath, but I heard it and so did Jeremy, who looked at his dad in surprise.

"Tom," Meg said.

"Bree, you don't have any idea how dangerous these people are," Hambecker said. "They'd kill you as soon as look at you."

"Why don't you guys tell me who they are and then I won't have to figure it out by myself?" I was mad that they were holding out on me. I didn't care if their jobs required it. I was mad anyway.

"Because I'm afraid if you write about this they'll target you. I'd rather you left it alone." Tom sounded sad, which somehow made me even angrier. I could take care of myself, damn it. He didn't need to get all *sad* on me.

"Bree, the paper is not worth getting yourself killed over. Please." Meg made big eyes at me, which I thought meant we could talk about it later, but I was too far gone.

"I'm not leaving it alone. And damn *yes*, I'm going to write about it. People want to know about this stuff. According to you, there are dangerous criminals murdering people in our town. We deserve to know who it is." I stood up, dropping my napkin on the table. "I have to go," I said. I looked at Meg. "Sorry to eat and run."

I stomped across the door yard to my truck and wrenched the door open.

"Bree! Wait." Meg jogged over. "This is my fault. I should have warned you."

"Duh."

"Listen, I know you're doing this for the paper. But it's not worth it. Tom and Richard are concerned. They think you could be in real trouble." She had her hand on my arm.

"Would Lucy give up? I don't think so. The paper needs this. *I* need this."

Meg dropped her hand from my arm. "Bree, I know I've been kind of bitchy lately, but if it comes down to a choice, I'd rather have you than the paper. I can always find another job. I can't find another you."

"I still can't let this go, Meg. I just can't. I want this story. For me."

I got in the truck and watched her walk back into the house.

Jim was wearing form-fitting jeans and a blazer over a tight white T-shirt when he came to get me Sunday morning. I reminded myself that he couldn't be counted on when things got tough, and got in the car. It wasn't a bad thing to be hanging out with a handsome and attentive guy, but I needed to remember why I was there and not lose my head in a flood of memories. If I wasn't careful I'd remember what a jerk he been and pop him one.

"So," I said as we took the on ramp to I-89 South, "how have things been?" Could I get any lamer?

"Pretty good. I had some stuff hanging over me, but that's all tied up now. I'm free to enjoy the day. I'm glad you decided to come with me. I miss having someone to go to the races with."

"I thought Lucy liked going to the races."

"Lucy was after only one thing, and it wasn't sex. When I refused to give her information about my cases, she moved on. We were never really together."

There was no telling what Lucy's opinion was about that. She was not my favorite person, and I thought she'd probably been using Jim for the twin purposes of getting back at me and furthering her career. I doubted she'd ever had real feelings for Jim. In fact I doubted she'd ever had any feelings at all.

"What kind of things did you have hanging over your head?" I asked, hoping I sounded conversational and not like I was giving him the third degree.

"Every once in a while I get a client that I also know personally. Mixing my private life and business makes me extremely uncomfortable."

Don't I know it, I thought.

"I finally got the details worked out and the case off my desk, so the tension hasn't got me all ratcheted up anymore. That's always a good thing."

I should have known he wouldn't give up any details; he wasn't a partner in his firm for nothing.

"Can we stop at Panera on the way?" I asked. "I want a chocolate croissant."

We listened to alternative rock the rest of the way to Loudon. He knew better than to try and impress me with classical. Not that I'm an anti-classical snob, it's just that Jim's taste in music tends to make me sleep. I like to sing when I'm in the car.

Jim used his connections and got us a parking spot in the VIP lot. We ambled past tailgaters grilling burgers and hot dogs. He held my hand as we bypassed the entrance gate and wandered into the parking area reserved for booths, games, advertisers and other forms of entertainment. A band of rockers from the eighties were playing their oldies hits to a crowd of race fans. The army recruiters had an obstacle course set up and one of the cadets dared me to test my strength. I passed. No way was I going to make a fool of myself out there in front of everybody and their mother.

The music made it hard to talk to Jim, and I couldn't walk five feet without someone trying to get me to sign up for some gimmick or other, so I was relieved when he led me back to the gates to the track. We had seats up high in the stands, just beneath the indoor suites on the first turn. Not the most expensive seats in the place, but the ones with the best view, in my opinion anyway.

Jim's sleeve brushed against my shoulder on our way up the stairs. My body tingled with awareness and I was intimately reminded of how much I used to like to touch him, damn it. *Get your head together. This guy could be a murderer.* But he didn't feel like a murderer. He felt warm and solid and very *there*. I could feel myself morphing into the *I don't care what rotten thing you did to me, I'm going to sleep with you anyway* Bree. But the fact he was good in bed was not a good enough reason to compromise my principals. I just had to keep reminding myself of that.

The racecars were lined up down pit row, according to starting position. The drivers had headed down to the podium where they would be announced and then be ferried around the track in a pick up while waving to the fans.

I stood up.

"I'll be right back."

I trotted down the steps and made my way to the ladies' room where I did what I needed to do and held my wrists under the cold water. I filled my hands. The water stung when I splashed it on my face. I leaned on the counter and watched the water drip off my face in the mirror. It was far too hot.

I saw movement behind me and turned to see a blond in cut-offs and a midriff baring tank staring at me. "It's no wonder you're hot," she said. "You've got too many clothes on." She swung her backside into the far stall and I looked back at my reflection but I didn't have any words of wisdom for myself. Apparently having a red face with water dripping from it leaves you open to comments from strangers.

"Shit," I said, "I am over dressed," and made my way back to the stands.

There was a skinny, thin-faced guy sitting in my seat talking earnestly to Jim when I got back up the stands. I stood on the steps and wondered if I should give them space or demand my seat back. An excited voice announced the start of the race over the PA system, so I started past the fans to my seat, but Jim and Mr. Weasel Face stood up and came toward me so half way there I had to turn around.

"Make up your mind, lady."

"Sorry. I'm sorry."

I noticed that neither Jim nor the guy he was with bothered to say anything. Why is it only women who feel the need to apologize for their actions?

The loudspeaker roared "Start Your Engines," and everyone in the stands stood up. I didn't know what the guy wanted, but whatever it was, we were going to miss the start of the race.

The growl of engines made it impossible to

communicate so Jim motioned me to follow and we made our way down the stands and back out into the parking lot. The guy was almost a foot shorter than me and when Jim started to go the wrong way he had to tug on Jim's arm to get his attention. It was like following Sheldon and Leonard.

We made our way to a motorhome on the hill behind the track reserved for camping. The guy opened the door and ushered us inside. The race noise was considerably muted inside and I thought the rig must have special noise-reducing walls. I could even hear the hum of the air conditioning. It was dark and cool and the air smelled of old beer. Clearly a guy's RV. I almost didn't see Grant Foster in a grungy t-shirt sitting slouched in the dinette.

"Oh, hi," I said.

The weasel said something to Jim that sounded like "girl plant steak, pervert Guinness," which I translated to mean, "Girl can't stay, private business." I headed toward the door.

"Bree. You can stay." Jim caught me by the arm.

Weasel Man's face turned red, "But…"

"She stays until I deem it prudent for her to leave." He had my hand tight in his now.

"But…" Weasel guy was sputtering.

"Believe me; she'll get in far worse trouble out there than in here." He was moving me toward the table.

"Jim!" I hated it when he insinuated I would get myself in trouble if not watched.

"Listen, Willard, she's with me. If she goes, I go. Do you need my advice or not?" He stopped and when Willard didn't immediately respond he turned for the door.

"Fuck. Fine."

Jim motioned me to sit and slid in next to me. Willard the weasel sat next to Grant, who seemed as if he might be hung over. Maybe he partied with someone else last night. But then I thought about it and couldn't remember him drinking a single beer or mixed drink.

"Hey Bree," he said to me. "Seems like yesterday." He managed a feeble grin.

"Grant, this is James Fisk," Willard the weasel cut in. "He's a lawyer."

"Grant Fraser." He stuck his hand out for Jim to shake across the table.

"Tell me Grant, why am I in a beer-soaked RV instead of sitting with my date at the races?"

He deflated, sinking back into the brown upholstered cushions. "Some kind of trouble. I got a phone call telling me to throw the big cup race next weekend."

"Who told you to throw the race?" Jim asked.

"I'm not sure. There was this woman. French I think. Margaret something."

French. My heart pounded faster. There were too many coincidences.

"Willard," He nodded to the weasel. "Is my business manager, he said I should tell you what happened. I don't know if I should take it seriously or not."

"When did this happen?"

"For God's sake, what does that matter?" Willard was wild eyed and agitated.

"Let him answer my questions." Jim laid his hand on Willard's arm and Willard jumped. "Take it easy."

"After the race in Kentucky." Grant said. "I got a call on my cell."

"What did she say?" Jim asked. I could feel him tapping his foot under the table.

"If I throw the race she'll pay me $50,000. As if! I told her no way in hell." Grant's voice was low and angry. If you'd have asked me at the bar I would have said he never lost his temper.

"That's it. She offered to bribe you?" Jim had taken out a pocket notebook and was scribbling in it.

"No. When I told I don't take bribes, she showed up at the RV."

That sounded like a predator to me. Separate your prey from the pack.

"I told her no again, and she said fine, I'd just saved her fifty thou, but if I don't throw the race, she'll kill me."

"Why don't you just withdraw? Get the flu. Or contact the race authorities?"

"I had some, uh, incidents last year. If I screw up, I'll lose my job. And the crew, man, they are so excited. We could win this race."

"So what? Find another job," Jim said.

I looked at Jim. *What the hell?* More pressure on my foot. Apparently he thought he knew what he was doing.

"This team is my last hope. The owner took a huge chance on me. I throw this race I might as well kill myself." Grant ran his hand through his hair.

"Better dead than alive but not racing?" Jim asked.

"Pretty much." Grant said. "I mean it's hokey, but racing is my life."

Jeez, talk about screwed up priorities.

"Hey, now, Grant. That's no way to be talking. We can sort this out." Willard the weasel rubbed Grant's shoulder and for a second it reminded me of Gollum with Frodo, kind of creepy.

"No, we can't, Willard. She knew who to target. I'm dead."

"That's why I got Jim here. He's a lawyer, he can help."

Jim looked at me. "Maybe this would be good time for you to get some fresh air. There could be confidentiality issues." Jim slid out of the booth. I followed. I searched for something encouraging and appropriate to say but nothing surfaced from the recesses of my brain so I just let myself out.

I sat on the steps and strained my ears. Couldn't hear a thing from inside the RV. "Damn!"

I wandered toward the track hoping to see some of the race. There was an old sap bucket with a rusty rim next to the steps of the RV closest to Grant's. I walked past it, looking to see a beer can floating in ten inches of water; the leftovers from last night's ice bucket. Across the tarmac the race leaders flew around turn two and the growl made me wince. I pulled earplugs from my pocket and shoved them in my ears. I love racecars, but they are freaking loud when you aren't the one driving.

A hand on my shoulder made me jump and I spun to see Jim at my side. He slid an arm around my shoulder and steered me back down the hill.

"What's up?" I asked behind the stands, where at least you could hear yourself think.
"Did you solve his problem?"

"I think he's going to the race officials. That was my second piece of advice anyway."

"What was so confidential about that?" I asked.

"I didn't want you implicated if he told me he was doing something illegal. If you didn't hear it, then you aren't responsible for doing anything about it."

"Right. Good idea." I followed Jim back to the stands feeling a squishiness in my stomach that had started at the mention of a French woman and gotten worse from there. I climbed the endless stairs and sidled past the fans to our seats. There was no talking over the noise of the engines, not that I had anything to say.

The race was uneventful, not that I would have noticed much. My mind was fixated on one thing: A man that I would consider pretty much fearless—you had to be to race cars—was afraid for his life because of a French woman who might or might not be Margaret, and could possibly be Michèle. Not that Michèle had done anything but cry all over the place, but still. Everywhere I looked—too many coincidences. It unnerved me.

"Come on, Bree," Jim said when the race was over. "I'm taking you home."

"Wait, did my driver win?"

"He came in second. Are you feeling all right?"

"Yeah. I'm fine." *If you don't count the fact that something is not adding up.*

"Do you think it's a coincidence," I asked Jim on the way home. "A guy shows up dead at Planet Hair, and now Grant is being threatened?"

"I don't see what they could have in common." He had his eyes on the road. "Am I missing something?"

"That's a lot of violence to suddenly show up in

one place." I was pretending to watch the road in front of us, but I out of the corner of my eye I was gauging his reaction.

"It didn't show up in the same place. Grant was nowhere near South Royalton when he was threatened." There was no tension in his face, he just looked tired.

"But he's *from* South Royalton." I was turned in my seat, focused on him, but he wouldn't look my way. I wasn't getting any love here.

"Coincidence," he said.

"Have you heard any more about the murder?" I asked. "Any clues?"

"Anything I hear, I'll tell the police. If they want you to know they can tell you."

"Really, you won't tell me anything?"

"I don't know anything to tell you, Bree. Can we talk about something else?" Tiny lines appeared next to his eyes. "I like not to be at work for a while. How are your dogs?"

It made for a long trip home, me wanting to ask questions about the murder, Jim not wanting to answer. I gave up and took a nap.

"Why don't you come to my place?" Jim asked as we drove into Royalton. "I've got beer."

"Yeah, why not?" There were very good reasons why not, but if I saw the pants in the closet after I'd been invited in Tom could use that to get a search warrant.

"Want to stay for dinner? I can fire up the grill." He was more relaxed now.

"What are you making?" My stomach was growling, and I would have eaten just about anything, but it seemed polite to ask.

CRAZY LITTLE THING CALLED DEAD

"Steak. Grilled with mushrooms and peppers." He smiled as he turned up his road. "Ice cream."

I could never resist ice cream.

"Sounds good. Yeah, I'll stay." I felt a little shame-faced. Here Jim was making dinner for me, and here I was spying on him. I didn't even think finding out he was a murderer would make me feel better. There are some things you just don't want to know about your ex.

"Make yourself comfortable. I'll be back in a sec." He stepped out onto the back deck.

"I'm gonna use the bathroom," I called after him.

"Help yourself."

I went down the hall, past the closet of the offending pants and shut myself in the bathroom. I stood there, leaned against the door and breathed. I was having trouble justifying searching Jim's closets when he could catch me at it. But that was the point, I'd been invited in. I took a deep breath and stepped out of the bathroom.

I went straight to the closet and opened the door. I rifled through the jackets where I remembered the suit pants hanging, and there they were. Now Steve could get a search warrant.

"What are you doing?"

I jumped and turned to find Jim standing behind me. "Oh, uh, I thought maybe we could eat outside, but it's cool. I was borrowing a jacket." I flipped past the Burberry—unsuitable for an informal occasion—and pulled out a fleece. "This should fit me."

Yeah, right. I was wearing a fleece dress. But I shoved up the sleeves and smiled at him.

"No seriously Bree. What are you doing in my closet?"

"I told you what I was doing in your closet.

Borrowing a fleece." I performed a flourish with both hands sweeping the length of the sweater like I was on Let's Make a Deal or something.

He gave me a look that said he didn't believe me for a minute and stood stone faced.

"All right." I pulled the pants from the closet. "Where'd these come from? They look just like the jacket Albin Shvakova was wearing."

"Albin Shvakova? What are you talking about?"

"You know. The dead guy at Planet Hair."

Jim threw his head back and laughed until there were tears in his eyes. "My God," he said, choking back the laughter, "you thought I killed the guy? That's a good one, even for you. Wait until I tell my partners. This will be good for a dinner or two out."

"How do you explain the pants, then?" My cheeks were hot and I'd rather be just about anywhere but here, still I wouldn't let it go.

"You don't remember?" Jim looked at me, eyebrows up. "Halloween, two years ago. The Halloween dance on the Green? I went as a hobo."

The truth dawned on me and I felt ridiculous. I'd seen him there; in fact we'd danced together. The bottoms of the pant legs had ended mid-ankle and he'd kept them up with frayed rope. The pants were part of his costume. I stood there, mortified, with no idea what to do next. *How the hell do I get myself out of here?*

"Come on," Jim threw his arm around my shoulders, "let's go eat. I haven't laughed like that in a long time. You have some nerve, I'll give you that."

He led me down the hall and out onto the porch. "You really should stop letting your imagination get the better of you," he said. "It's going to get you in trouble. But jeez," he swiped at his eyes with his free hand.

"That's hilarious."

We sat on the deck swing and watched the river. Jim's arm was around my shoulder and I hoping he wasn't going to ask me to sleep with him. I was trying to figure out how to ask him to take me home already, without seeming rude. But no matter how I phrased it in my head, it sounded bad. Jim pulled me in close and dropped a kiss on the spot where my shoulder met my neck and I jumped up and moved away.

"Could you take me home now? I've got barn chores." I tried to sound contrite, but I don't think I quite got there. More panicked than apologetic.

"Sorry. I shouldn't have kissed you. It was just so comfortable sitting here with you." He stood up. "I'll take you home."

We were just stepping out the door when the black Escalade pulled up in the door yard. I was kind of surprised; I didn't know Hambecker knew where Jim lived. We walked out and met him as he angled out of his truck.

"There you are," Hambecker said to me. "I was wondering where you got to. Maverick needs you down at the barracks."

"What's he need Bree for?" Jim kicked right in to confrontational lawyer mode.

"I don't mind," I said. "You can drop me there instead of taking me all the way home."

"You shouldn't speak to the police without a

lawyer present," Jim said. "That's the first thing I teach my clients. I'll go in with you." He put a protective arm across my shoulder, and I could almost see Hambecker mentally rolling his eyes.

I slid out from under the arm. "Are you headed to the barracks?" I asked Hambecker.

"Yeah. You want to catch a ride?" Hambecker looked relieved.

"Perfect," I said. "That'll save Jim a trip." I gave Jim a quick hug to mollify him, backing away almost before he could hug me back. "Thanks for taking me to the races. Don't look like that, it's Tom. He's not going to arrest me."

I got in the SUV and we pulled out, leaving Jim standing in his door yard looking a little like someone had stolen his thunder.

"Listen to this," I said. "Remember Grant Fraser from the other night?"

Hambecker nodded his assent.

"A French woman threatened to have him killed if he doesn't throw the race next weekend." I rolled down the window and let the cool air flow over me.

"Is he going to do it?" He rolled the window back up with the controls in his door. "I've got the air conditioner on."

"I don't know. Jim wouldn't let me hear that part of the conversation. I had to go out and wander the parking lot." I cracked the window an inch.

Hambecker sighed, turned off the a/c and rolled all four windows down. "Is that better?"

"Yes. Thank you." I meant to give him a polite smile, but I couldn't control my mouth and ended grinning.

"Jim's right though. It's better if you don't know. If

you weren't present you can't be implicated if there's an inquiry." He smiled and glanced over at me. "He was protecting you."

Huh. What do you know?

"Don't you think it's odd that Grant was threatened by a woman with a French accent, and the woman who wants me to find her boyfriend also has a French accent?" I rested my arm on the door and let the wind play over my hand.

"Why ask you to find her boyfriend? You're not a private investigator." He rubbed a hand over his head.

"No. Apparently half the town told her I'm nosy enough for the job, so she picked me." I hadn't thought about it much at the time, but now it kinda hurt. I'm not nosy, just curious.

"Did you agree?" He turned up my road and we bounced over the ruts the town hadn't graded yet. My road was always the last to be repaired.

"What? That I'm nosy? Not really, but she wouldn't take no for an answer. Left a bunch of money on my desk. And now Grant's been threatened by a French woman as well," I said.

"It is an interesting coincidence. What was the name of the woman who hired you?" Hambecker turned into my drive and cut the engine.

"Michèle Ledroit. Grant thought the woman who threatened him was Margaret."

"Margaret LeDonne." Hambecker said under his breath.

"Who?" I asked.

"Margaret LeDonne. She's a consigliore for a family in New York City. Normally a consigliore remains on the right side of the law, but she's known to run rackets of her own. I doubt she has anything to do

105

with you or Grant. She doesn't usually go after small fish." He was watching my face, gauging my level of comprehension, I thought.

I considered taking offense at being called a small fish for about ten seconds, then I let it go. I wouldn't exactly call myself a big fish.

Chapter Eight

"You don't think Michèle Ledroit and Margaret LeDonne are the same person?" I could hear my dogs barking inside the house, so I opened the SUV door, wanting to go let them out.

"I highly doubt it. And whoever threatened Grant, I don't think it was Margaret LeDonne. There are a million Margarets in the world. If Grant remembered the name right in the first place. Some people aren't good with details."

"I've got to let the dogs out before one of them goes through a window," I said.

Hambecker got out of the car and followed me to the door. "Regardless of who is making the threats I don't want you taking any chances. Don't assume anyone is harmless, and don't turn your back." He took my jaw gently and looked me in the eye. "It's important, Bree, you need to pay attention."

The attraction I felt for him was magnified at close quarters. His touch on my face was warm and distracting. I wanted more, much, much more, and I was imagining what the more might be.

"Bree?" His eyes were close. I could see flecks of gold mixed in with the green and brown.

"I know, pay attention." I opened the door and let the dogs surge between us.

The next morning I sat in the empty office working on the dead guy piece with oatmeal and hot Earl Grey on my on my desk. Tea isn't usually my beverage of choice but even I need a break from coffee now and then. The oatmeal could have been my nod to healthy living, except that I loaded it with chocolate chips so it was kind of like eating warm cookies. I was just testing the temperature of the tea when the phone rang.

"Royalton Star," I said in my best business voice. No reason to let my lack of business acumen chase even more clients away. Rasping came over the line.

"Hello?" I said.

"You need to leave it alone." He was a cross between Darth Vader and Batman.

"I'm sorry, I couldn't quite hear you." This was kind of interesting; I'd never had a crank caller before.

"Leave it alone. You know what I mean." Again with the Batman voice.

I resisted the urge to laugh. "No. I don't know what you mean. Are you sure you have the correct number?"

"Leave it alone." There was some Darth Vader breathing and he hung up.

I looked at the receiver. "That had to be the most bizarre phone call ever." I put the phone in its cradle and drank some tea.

Not long after I heard steps on the stairs. I looked at the time; it was too early for it to be Meg or Deirdre. And it wasn't. Michèle Ledroit walked in the door looking as if she'd just walked out of a Paris salon.

"I haven't heard from you," she said. "I thought by now you would have found Victor."

"Look, I'm sorry. I haven't had time to really search for Victor. I'm researching a murder."

She burst into tears and I wanted to smack my forehead.

"I can give you a reward." She sniffed and dropped a stack of money on my desk.

The top bill was a Franklin and I wondered if they were all the same. The barely functional tires on my truck came to mind. I was pretty sure that stack of money would get me four new tires and a spare. *Focus, Bree.*

"I can't accept that," I said. "I may never find Victor Puccini."

"Please? I'll pay you for looking," Her tears were everywhere, dropping off her nose and chin. "If you find him I can give you a bonus. Please?"

I passed her the tissues.

"Not to be rude or anything, but why me? Why not the state police?"

"I do not trust the police."

"I'm really sorry; I don't have time to go looking right now. I'm in the middle of an assignment." *And to tell the truth, I'm pretty sure I don't want anything to do with you. I see you crying, but I'm not feeling your pain.*

She started sobbing. "But what if the murder and Victor are connected. If you find him then you might know everything." At least I think that's what she said. She was nearly incoherent.

Ho boy. This woman is loony 'toons.

Michèle left the bills on my desk and rose. When she got to the door she turned and looked at me for a moment.

She sniffed again, and wiped her eyes.

"I'm afraid what might happen if you don't find him. Something bad. He could be hurt."

Right. Also, over-protective.

"I'm afraid, please find Victor Puccini."

She left the door open as she left, descending the stars quietly.

A drill jackhammered in my head. I tapped on my keyboard, searching Michèle Ledroit. Nothing showed up that made sense to me. I picked up the phone and dialed Tom. He told me he'd look into her. I sat for a moment, willing my heart rate to drop.

When the answer to my query came it wasn't in the form of a phone call. Heavy footsteps sounded on the stairs and before I could work myself into a state of high anxiety, Tom came in through the open door. I'd forgotten to close it. He sat in the chair that Michèle Ledroit had occupied earlier, stretching his legs out to the side of my desk.

"Tell me about this woman." He was watching me.

"She came in here crying the day after the murder. Said her boyfriend, Victor Puccini, was missing and that it was his car that went into the lake." I shrugged.

"That car belonged to Margaret LeDonne." Tom tapped one finger on my desktop.

"Maybe Victor Puccini was driving it?"

Tom reached up and slid the card off my desk from where it had been sitting next to where Ledroit had left the pile of Franklins. He flipped the card over and over in her hand.

Tom rested his elbows on my desk, leaning into me. "Ledroit comes in here the first time, turns on the water works and begs you to find her boyfriend. The second time she cries even harder and then tells you he's in danger? I've got that right?"

"Pretty much. And she offered me money. That stack of Franklins." I pointed to the money I'd yet to touch.

"How do you feel about lying low for a while? Maybe going to visit your folks? Or better still, don't you have a brother in California?" He was tapping the card on my desk now. "I'm going to take this away with me. I'll bring it back later. You weren't thinking of calling her, were you?" This was not a question.

"The woman is loony 'toons. I don't think she's dangerous. And why is it whenever anything gets hinky, cops ask me to leave town? It gives me the distinct feeling that you don't want to deal with me."

"If you weren't such a busybody…"

"No you don't. You are not pinning this on me. Just because I happened to be present when Claire found the body…"

"That's exactly what I mean. You see a body and instead of running the other way you go and see if the guy is alive. If you weren't a busybody you'd be running the other direction as fast as you could. Not leaving fingerprints all over the place for me to explain to my boss. As far as he's concerned, you're a rare female serial killer. If we had any spare officers he'd have you under surveillance." Tom rubbed his hand across his close-cropped hair. "But knowing what you're like, all I'm asking is that you call for help if anything strange shows up on your radar. Can you do that for me?"

"Sure thing, boss."

Tom wasn't gone thirty minutes when Hambecker walked in. I hadn't heard footsteps on the stairs so when the door came flying open I jumped about three feet.

"What's the matter, Trouble, not expecting company?" he asked. The words were light but I thought I could hear tension underlying them.

"What'd you do? Levitate up the stairs? Give a girl some warning next time."

"Didn't realize I was in stealth mode. Sorry about that." He stood in front of my desk. "I'm heading out to Thetford. Want to tag along? I'm asking in the spirit of cooperation, not out of any need to keep an eye on you."

"I was just in Thetford," I said. I cringed internally, thinking Hambecker might not be too happy about it. "It might look weird if I showed up again with you."

"You already went to Thetford." His voice was hard. "Why am I not surprised? You are fucking going to get yourself killed one of these days, and I am not going to be able to do a damn thing about it."

He was back out the door before I could respond. My heart was pounding and there was a suspicious stinging behind my eyes. It had happened so fast that I wasn't sure what I was reacting to. I reached over to grab a tissue and my hand was shaking. I wished I'd lied to Hambecker so I could be safe in his black SUV listening in on his questions. Not sitting here dealing with sobbing strangers and cranky bosses.

I threw my oatmeal in the trash and went home to cry in private.

I gave in and rolled my motorcycle out of the barn.

The evening was warm and clear, no rain in the forecast. I pulled on my helmet and headed into town watching carefully for stray fawns. I loved how the air changed temperature as I drove down the hill, and then caught me with cool dampness as I rode across the river. By the time I got to Meg's place, my mood had changed and I was feeling much mellower.

But when I got to the kitchen door I stopped. I could hear laughter; one of the kids was howling with glee. Usually, I'd open the door and join right in, but although I was calmer, I wasn't in the mood for the kind of ruckus I heard behind the door. I turned and walked along the porch and onto the deck overlooking the river. The grill was set up near the railing and I peeked under the hood to see what was there. Several steaks were sizzling away but they weren't ready to be turned. I leaned on the rail and watched the river. It is close enough to see a canoe gliding along but not close enough that I could tell who was in it.

I felt someone lean on the rail next to me and looked to see Hambecker. I sighed involuntarily and regretted it. Better not to let him know that he got under my skin.

"Can we call a truce for the evening?" he asked.

"You yelled at me." The words still stung.

"I know." His eyes were on the river, but he was still close enough to that I could smack him. And boy, did I want to smack him.

"That's it? I know?" My face felt hot and I had to remind myself to breathe.

"Crap, Bree, you get me so wound up I don't know what I'm saying half the time." He was looking at me now, but I was having a hard time meeting his eyes.

"Is that your idea of an apology? Because if it is, it

113

sucked." I looked at the smooth boards of the deck under my feet wanting to end the argument, not being able to back down.

"Hell." He took a minute to breathe. "I realize it's your job to investigate stories, and I shouldn't interfere." He touched my face and gently lifted my chin so I was looking him in the eye. "I'm sorry I yelled at you."

I stood there and blinked at him like an idiot. Not one appropriate word came to mind. All I could think was if I leaned in just a little bit I'd be able to kiss him. Where was my righteous indignation when I needed it?

"Bree?" He dropped my chin and took a step back. "Are you with me here?"

"Uh, yeah." *I accept your apology and raise you one night of passion.* "Thank you. We should go in now."

"That's it? Thank you, and we should go in now? What the hell is wrong with you?" He turned and went inside, slamming the door behind him.

"Me?" I yelled even though I knew he couldn't hear me. "What the hell is wrong with *you*?" *Fucking apologizing and gazing in my eyes one minute, and yelling and stomping into the house the next.* I stopped myself from yelling 'asshole', but only just. That man brought out the very worst in me. I was going to have to pull myself together or go home. I opened the grill and started flipping steaks. This at least, I knew how to do.

Tom came out and joined me at the grill.

"Turn that one, there," he said, pointing.

"I'll get to it. You abandoned the grill now you have to deal with grilling the MacGowan way." I kept my eyes on the grill, mortified by the tears in my eyes.

"Actually, Hambecker was doing the grilling. He asked me to take over but it looks like you've got it handled." He sat down on the bench behind me.

I closed the lid on the grill and leaned my elbows on the railing. What was wrong with me that I couldn't get along with anyone? I'd been yelled at worse than that on several occasions. Why was I letting it bother me this time? That damn Hambecker had me all messed up. The pressure in my head was building to the point I just wanted to bang my head against a tree. I wished Tom would go away so I could have a good cry and get over it.

"What's up with you, MacGowan? You aren't usually a brooder." Now it was Tom with his forearms on the railing next to me.

"If you mean I don't sit on eggs, you'd be right. This whole talking thing could use some work though." I sighed and put my back to the river.

"What's going on?" He nudged me. "Having a lovers spat?"

"Hambecker. One minute I think he likes me, the next minute he's shouting orders at me." I looked at my feet. My boots were scuffed.

"Doesn't know what to do with you. I have that problem too. In a slightly different way, of course." There was warmth in his voice, and a smile. It reminded me of my brother, JW.

"Doesn't give him the right to yell at me." I moved back to the grill and flipped the steaks again. Dusk was starting to settle in.

"Do me a favor; let it go for the evening. Meg's frazzled and she doesn't need any extra doom and destruction at the moment." He put a fatherly hand on my shoulder.

"Okay." I sighed again. It was getting to be a habit.

"Good, now help me get this meat on a plate so we

can eat. I'm starved."

I held the plate while Tom pulled steaks off the grill. He opened the door for me so I could carry the meat into the kitchen.

I sat at the table with Jeremy on one side of me and Sara on the other. Hambecker was across the table from me so I kept my eyes on my plate. I forked steak, baked potato and salad onto my plate, asked Sara for the dressing and busied myself eating. Eating without looking at the person across from you is fine if you don't mind appearing rude. I kept imagining I could feel Hambecker's eyes on me.

"Bree can I borrow Beans for a school project?" Sara was looking at me like I held her future in my hands.

"Beans is your Uncle Beau's dog, sweetie. You'll have to ask him. Eat your dinner now." I pointed my fork at her meat. "Or I can take care of it for you."

"Uncle Beau said I have to ask you because you'll have all the inconvenience." She piled lettuce on top of her steak.

"Did he really say it was all right with him? Or is this one of those things where you tell me he said it was okay, and then you go to him and tell him I said it was okay, and we both agree because we each thought the other one said yes, and then you get your way?" I uncovered her steak and cut it in half. "Start with that."

"He really did say I had to ask you. Didn't he, Mom?" Sara tuned to look at her mother, but Meg was dumping sour cream on her potato.

"I'm sorry Sara, I wasn't paying attention. What did you say?" Meg asked.

"Uncle Beau told me to ask Bree about Beans." Sara pushed the steak to the far side of her plate.

"Yeah. that's true." Meg said, cutting her steak into peanut sized pieces.

"Then it's a done deal." I said. "When do you need him?"

"Tomorrow. Mom said she'd call before you left home, but she forgot." The steak was now halfway off Sara's plate and Hambecker reached across the table, snagged it with his fork and added it to his plate. I looked up to see him grimacing at her a finger to his lips. She giggled.

"I'll take you up after dinner and you can help me gather up his stuff." I said, taking a bite. The steak was good despite the haphazard grilling it had gotten.

"What are you going to do with Beans at school, Sara?" Hambecker asked. "Isn't that against the rules?"

"We're doing a unit on responsibility. We have to have be responsible for an entire week." Sara was hacking her potato into little pieces now.

"Are you going to eat any of that?" I asked under my breath.

"I had a sammich before dinner. Don't tell mom." She hissed back.

"Wow," Hambecker interrupted our exchange, "will you take him with you every day?"

"For the first day. Then we just have them at home and keep a journal about it. Mom said she could help make sure I don't forget to feed or water him." She palmed some potato and fed it to Mooch Dog under the table.

"Your Mom's going to kill you if she catches you doing that," I whispered.

Tom looked up and caught Sara's eye. "Your Mom's busy, short stuff. I expect you to do the job and not make your mother nag you."

117

"I'll do it right, Dad. I've got a plan." Sara's fork was frozen half way to her hand. She put it in her mouth instead.

Meg placed a hand on Tom's arm. "It's fine, Tom. Sara's project is not a hardship."

They looked at each other for a moment, until he nodded. "Of course Sara's project isn't a hardship. It'll be fun to have Beans here for a while. But just out of curiosity why not one of our dogs?"

"Duh. Mom takes care of our dogs." Sara said, her hand full of potato again was sliding under the table. I'll give her one thing, the girl had nerve.

"Right." Tom went back to his steak and Meg dropped her hand from his arm, the train wreck diverted.

However, there was a lot of slobbering coming from under the table.

I lay on the bed, fully dressed, with my face in the pillow. The dogs were sprawled on the floor in my room, I could hear panting and the occasional shift in position. Annabelle Cat reclined, diva like, on the other pillow. Her tail smacking me every so often.

"Go away, Annabelle Cat. You're interrupting my meditative funk."

Her tail hit me again. Crap. Without lifting my head I reached over and swatted at her with my hand. Annabelle Cat pounced on me, sinking her claws and fangs into my hand.

"Hey!" I jerked my hand back and rolled over checking the damage. Two sets of claws and teeth. I must have really pissed her off. I got off the bed and went to disinfect my hand in the downstairs bathroom where I kept the first aid kit, but the dog started barking and when I got to the kitchen Hambecker was standing at my door.

I let him in and he slouched into a kitchen chair, legs kicked out.

"Thirsty? I've got beer and soda." I headed for the fridge.

"Regular or diet soda?" He asked.

"I've got both." I held up two cans for his approval.

"Give me a regular."

I grabbed a cola out of the fridge and tossed it to him, then I popped a diet orange for me. I'd decided to cut down on caffeine. "Is this a social call?" I stood with my back to the sink and sipped soda off the top of the can. Beagle Annie came to lie at my feet.

Hambecker took a swig. "Not entirely, I need to talk to a suspect and I think it will go better if I have a woman with me."

"Aren't there any female agents around? Wouldn't that be normal procedure?" I poured some chips into a bowl and set it on the table.

"Bree, you're local. She may not know you, but she knows *of* you. The more relaxed she is the better this will go." He picked up a chip and tapped it on his can.

Then it occurred to me he was letting me listen in on a questioning and I should shut up and play along. "Just hand on a sec while I clean up my hand. Annabelle Cat took exception to me."

"Do you mind if I take my truck down as far as the

green?" I asked when I'd finished cleaning the bite. "I've got errands to do after."

I drove down the hill with Hambecker behind me eating my dust, which gave me a perverse kind of pleasure. I parked at the green and he pulled in next to me and got out.

"Why don't you jump in the truck? I'll be there in a minute."

I sat in the truck and wondered why he would ask me instead of getting another agent to go with him. Maybe he was going to do something that wasn't quite kosher. That worried me a little, but not enough to get out of the truck.

Five minutes later Hambecker pulled himself up into the truck and backed out. He turned onto 110 and headed out toward Tunbridge, which kind of surprised me. We were going to Ronnie's house?

"Ronnie's not, um, I don't know how to say this." I cast about in my brain for the appropriate phrasing. "She's mentally challenged. She's like a naive ten year old. She doesn't see things like an adult. At least, that's what Claire told me."

"I know. She's on the Asperger's spectrum. I'll go easy with her, but I need to know what she knows. She could be in danger."

Pretty soon we were sitting uncomfortably in Ronnie Hart's living room waiting for her to stop serving refreshments and sit down. At least I was uncomfortable; who knew what was going on in Hambecker's brain. I was vacillating between asking for a tour of the house, complimenting her food and keeping my mouth shut. I was afraid I'd say something I shouldn't and she would know I'd broken into her house, which could have been awkward.

When she finally sat down I was sweating along my hairline. I was hot and nervous and wishing Hambecker hadn't asked me to come along. He smiled what seemed like a genuine smile, complimented the lemonade and cookies.

"Ronnie," he said, "you know that a man was killed at Planet Hair?" He was quiet, gentle with her.

"Yes, there was a man. He died." She looked stricken. "He was a bad man."

"Do you know what happened?" Hambecker was watching her closely.

The phone rang and I jumped about a mile.

"Can I get the phone?" Ronnie asked. Hambecker nodded his assent and she jumped up and ran into the kitchen.

"Hughie, why are you calling me?" She had a sing songy lilt to her voice. Had to be someone she knew well.

"No, I didn't." Thump. Was she kicking the wall?

"No, I won't." Thump.

I looked at Hambecker and he shrugged.

"Okay, Hughie, bye." She sighed so loudly we could hear her in the living room. She came back in the room, a ten year old in a thirty year old body. I found her faintly disturbing. And then felt ashamed of myself. She seemed perfectly nice.

"That was my brother, Hugo," she said. "He's funny."

"Do you know where your brother is?" Hambecker asked.

"Yes!" She sat on the edge of her chair as if in anticipation.

"Can you tell me where he is?" Hambecker was infinitely patient.

"No. Hugo said not to tell." She was still perfectly happy.

"Do you know what he does for a living?" he asked.

"Like for a job?" She bounced a little in her chair.

Hambecker nodded.

"Security, I think. And he's a driver too. Hughie is a good driver." She smiled and bounced.

"Do you know who he works for, who pays him?" He was sitting very still. Very calm.

I was about to jump out of my skin. This was like pulling teeth from a walrus.

"A lady. A nice lady. Not the bad man." Ronnie scowled to show how she felt about the bad man.

"Does Hugo come to see you?" I asked. "Do you see him often?"

She beamed. It was the delighted smile of a five year old and it gave me shivers. How could this woman live here alone? She was so vulnerable. "I see Hughie all the time."

"And the night of the murder? Did he stop that night?" Hambecker asked. We were double teaming her now.

"Yes. He--" The phone rang again. Ronnie jumped up.

"Hello? Hughie? No, Hughie. All right." She hung up with another sigh and came back in the room. "I have to go to work now. It was nice meeting you."

We left without protesting, and she waved happily at us from the door.

Hambecker had a furrow between his brows, and was tapping on the steering wheel. I could almost see the wheels turning.

"Is it only me?" I asked. "Or did it seem like the

house was bugged?"

"No, it's not only you. I'd bet my car that someone was listening in. The question is was the listener in the house with us?"

"You think Hugh was in the house?" I looked at him in surprise. "Why didn't you search it?"

"I have to tread very carefully. It can't be said I was taking advantage of a mentally incompetent witness. It needs to go slow." He pulled over and cut the lights before we were out of sight of the drive.

"What are we doing?" I asked, although I had a pretty good idea.

"Watching," he said. "Just watching."

KATE GEORGE

Chapter Nine

We waited by the side of the road in the afternoon sunshine for about ten minutes before Ronnie's van went by. She didn't give us a second look. A minute after that a beat-up, blue Chevy truck flew by.

"I thought so," Hambecker cranked over the SUV and pulled out onto the road.

"Where did he come from?" I asked. "The truck wasn't parked in the door yard."

"Hidden from view behind the shed. It's been there on and off since the murder." He followed at a leisurely pace, and I was surprised when the truck turned left and we turned right.

"Aren't you going to follow him?" I asked, turning to look out the back window. The truck disappeared around a curve. "He's getting away."

"I know where he's going. I'll catch up with him tomorrow." Hambecker was relaxed, one hand on the steering wheel, the other on the arm rest.

"How do you know where he's going?" I was seriously confused. I only knew about the brother because Lori had mentioned him. How did Hambecker find out?

"I've been keeping an eye on him for a while."

"How long a while?" I had the feeling Hambecker wasn't telling me everything he knew. "Since before the murder?"

"A while before the murder, yeah." His voice was

casual, like he didn't realize what a traitor he was.

"You've been watching Ronnie Hart's brother since before the murder and you didn't bother to tell me about him? What is that? You told me you'd share information."

"Ronnie's brother is in his own class, filed under People Bree MacGowan Is Not To Mess With. Understand?" The slightest edge was audible in his voice. Hambecker was not a happy camper.

"You cheated. The deal was, you'd tell me what you knew. You knew you weren't going to honor the deal when you made it. Big jerk." I slumped back in the seat and stared out the front window. I should have known he wouldn't play fair. The fact that I wasn't playing fair either, and I should just get over it occurred to me. But I didn't let that stop me from sulking.

"Listen, Trouble, nothing you do is going to make me feel guilty about trying to keep you safe. *Trying* being the operative word. There isn't a man on this earth who could keep you safe from yourself."

"Says you. I don't need a guy to keep me safe." Why was it, that whenever I spent too much time with Hambecker, I always ended up wanting to hit him?

"Says me. And I should know. Man! You are hard to deal with."

I sat in shocked silence waiting for the next jab, but it didn't come. He shut right up. It was like he was trying to do some form of in vehicle meditation while he drove, keeping his breathing slow and his body relaxed. A fucking Zen master.

I, on the other hand, was pissed off and tight as a drum. I knew I wouldn't win either a verbal or physical sparring contest with Hambecker, but I might be able to win a sneaky contest. The SUV was still carrying the

GPS I'd planted on it. I'd checked it out on my phone as we were talking. I'd bet anything that as soon as he left me Hambecker would be on Hugo's tail. And I would be on Hambecker's. Hah. I felt just a tad magnanimous.

"Did you learn anything from talking to Ronnie?" I asked. "Because I sure didn't."

"I learned that someone doesn't want her talking to us. That seems significant." There was no angry residue in his voice. He'd zenned it right away.

"And that someone is her brother. Or at least she thought it was her brother, so it probably was. Don't you think?" Now was the time to ply him with silly questions and make him think I was off track.

"It was her brother. I saw him as he drove past us," Hambecker said.

"Ronnie's brother, Hugo Hart—who would name their kid Hugo Hart? That's just cruel." I tumbled Hugo Hart around in my brain for a minute, but it didn't matter how I looked at it, it was a pitiless name. Up there with John John and Justin Credible.

"His mother? I don't see anything wrong with it. It's no worse than being named *pretty cheese*." He grinned, but didn't take his eyes off the road.

"Don't be making fun of my name, Hammie." I stressed his name. I was regretting ever telling him the origins of mine. "It's a perfectly good name and much better that Hugo Hart. You know there's something I've been wondering about, if the Bulgarian assassin was killed at Planet Hair, how come there was no blood? There should have been some blood somewhere, shouldn't there?"

"There was blood. A lot of it. CSI got pictures with the UV light. Someone scrubbed the place clean." He

127

looked at me. "You're not going to barf in my rig are you? Because if you are I'm pulling over."

"No, I don't barf from talking about blood. I have to see it." Men. So concerned about their cars. "Why don't blood stains ever go away?" I asked. "Why can't they be cleaned up?" I'd been wondering about this for a while.

"Hell, I don't remember. Something about the iron, or was it protein? I'm not a crime scene guy. I'm a chase them down and take them out guy. I make the blood stains." He grinned.

"That's just gross. Didn't your mother teach you better than to say things like that?" *Jeez.*

"My mother would have slapped me silly for saying that in the house." He laughed. "But I'm not in the house."

"Har, har. What's your plan for tomorrow?" I asked.

"I've got stuff to do. I won't be around tomorrow. You can go do your investigative reporter thing without worrying about me getting in your way." He winked at me.

"What was that? Did you just wink at me?" He had to have lost his mind.

"I did not wink at you. I had a twitch in my eye. I always get twitches when I'm around you. You're bad for my nervous system." There was suppressed laughter in his voice.

"For heaven's sake, grow up." I sat with my arms crossed until we reached my house. I did not understand Hambecker one bit. One minute he was yelling at me and the next he was winking and laughing. I was beginning to think he was schizophrenic.

I parked on the Green and walked across to the office and climbed the stairs, wondering what kind of mood Meg would be in today. She was on the phone when I walked in, and Deirdre's bag was at her desk, but she wasn't in the room. Meg's conversation was low and tense and when I walked to my desk she swiveled her chair so her back was toward me.

"That was rude. It wasn't like I was going to listen in." I sat and booted my computer, checking on the state of the paper and working on both the dead man story and a Tropical Storm Irene retrospective. The advantage of a story like that was that it could be run whenever we needed filler, and it would always be interesting to our readers.

I tried to ignore the edgy conversation from the other side of the room. I turned Pandora on low but the occasional phrase came my way, and it sounded bad. Meg could get tense about deadlines and printing, but I hadn't ever heard this tone out of her. Something was not right.

The phone slammed down, and Meg's chair whirled around to face me.

"My God. I'm going to kill that Lucy Howe."

"What'd she do now? Sell us down the river?" I found it hard to get too serious about Lucy. I had bigger fish to fry.

"She's telling people we're going under! Of course everyone and their mother are calling to cancel ads. I swear if she shows her face in this office I'm going to take it clean off her." Meg was vibrating with anger.

"What are we going to do?" I asked.

"What *you* are going to do is design an online

edition for us. What *I* am going to do is call all our advertisers and offer them two free months of ads online if they'll keep their ad in the print edition." She looked at the ceiling. "How long will it take you to get that done? A week, two weeks? I'll pay you to do that and find someone else to write the articles."

"Not Lucy."

"Of course not Lucy. Lucy is dead to me. Lucy had better watch her sneaky little back." Meg glowered at me and turned back to her computer.

"It'll take me a day to get it all set up," I said. "Then it will just be putting ads in - we should link them to our advertiser's web sites - and dropping in articles. Only I had something I was going to do today, can it wait for tomorrow?"

"That depends, if you start tomorrow can you get it online tomorrow? I want us up and running as fast as possible." She had the ad book open in front of her and her hand on the phone.

"Never mind, I'll do it before I go."

The first thing I did was to register *TheRoyaltonStar.com* as a domain name. I was figuring out hosting when Deirdre stuck her head in the door. She motioned me out the door.

"I'll be right back," I got up and strolled to the door.

"What?" I asked Deirdre as I closed the door behind me.

"Is Meg still in there? She was ranting and raving earlier, she threw a book across the room."

"She still there, but she's calmed down some. She's having me work on an online edition." *And still muttering under her breath, but at least she isn't throwing things.* "How's the paper coming, is there much work left to do?"

"It's done. We're leaving all the ads in rather than rework the whole thing. Meg says it's an act of good faith, but I think it's desperation. I'd never be able to get all that work on time, and where would we find the filler?"

"If I get the online template done, can you lay in the content? I'm trying to get somewhere, but I can't go until this is handled." I'd sneaked a peak at the GPS tracking site. Hambecker was on the move, heading south.

"I'll do you one better, get the domain and whatnot set up, and I'll design the template. Shouldn't take too long, and we can release the online edition tonight and the print paper will be in circulation tomorrow." Deirdre's face was a mask of concentration. Her brow furrowed. "We can make this work."

"And yet again you save my bacon. But the payoff is that if I'm right, the next article is going to be a doozy—not just "the dead guy is a Bulgarian assassin and we don't know what he was doing in the states," like this week." I was excited thinking about it. There were a lot of possibilities and I just needed to find out more of what Hambecker knew.

"Let's get her done, then." Deirdre squared her shoulders and walked into the office with me behind. Meg was on the phone, but this time it seemed that the conversation was rational, and possibly preventative instead of reactionary.

I spent about thirty minutes doing what I needed to do and passed the mess over to Deirdre to tame into submission. Then I wondered how to get out of the office without Meg thinking I was deserting her. When she hung up the next phone call I interrupted her.

"The online edition is coming together, and

Deirdre is taking over the final stages. I'm going to go now, okay? I'm not bugging out." Well I was, but I didn't was Meg to feel that way.

"Yeah, fine." She looked up at me. "About a quarter of the businesses I've talked to think Lucy's off her rocker. A quarter of them hadn't heard anything, and the other half believed her."

"Better than all of them believing her," I said, surreptitiously gathering my stuff.

"Seventy-five percent are jumping on the online free advertising opportunity. We'll need to drop an announcement in the print edition, but that shouldn't be too difficult. Go. Find me something else to up the ante." She waved me away.

I didn't dawdle. I got the heck out of there and on the road. Hambecker was already passing Springfield. He was at least an hour and a half ahead of me. Maybe more.

I hit the freeway and set the cruise control at seventy-five and crossed my fingers that I didn't pass a traffic control cop. I figured Hambecker would be doing at least seventy and I wanted to make up time if I could.

For the first half hour or so, I was buzzing with impatience. I figured we were headed for New York City, a good five-hour drive, and I was impatient - and worried about losing Hambecker. But my phone had bars, and the website showed me the location of the

GPS. I was kind of surprised there weren't any glitches in my plan.

I left Vermont behind and settled into the drive. I checked to see where Hambecker was, and set my phone to randomly play music. I was bored, but anxious. Not a happy combination on a long drive. I pulled into a rest stop and downloaded an audio book from the Internet.

That helped. I lost myself in the story and didn't think to check on Hambecker again until I reached New Haven. He was still headed into the city. I stopped at a Service Plaza, pulled my bag out from behind the seat and went in to use the facilities. I came out with a piece of pizza, a bag of chocolate and a milkshake.

I balanced the food on the roof, unlocked the truck and got in. My phone wasn't where I left it.

I got out, felt in all my pockets, then leaned into the cab of the truck and scanned the floor. Not there. I let out a big sigh, climbed off the seat of the truck, grabbed the keys and trudged back into the plaza. A search of all the places I'd been produced nothing. My phone was gone.

Back out at the truck I formulated a plan that factored in a quick trip to a city library to use the computers. I was about to pull back out onto the road when I noticed a guy waving and pointing at my roof.

"What?" I asked palms up.

He pointed to the roof again and it dawned on me. My pizza, milkshake and chocolate were still on the roof. I waved my thanks and retrieved my food. Jeez, I couldn't believe I almost lost my milkshake.

The worst part of losing my phone was that I didn't have my story to listen to. I turned on the radio, but it wasn't nearly as satisfying as losing myself in a novel. I took a sip of my milkshake and slid pizza out of its box. At least I wasn't going to starve to death.

The rest of the trip into the city was nerve-wracking. I just wasn't used to driving in traffic and there were cars everywhere. It took every nerve in my body not to turn around and go home. I pulled off the freeway in Brooklyn, looking for a place to ask directions and in the five seconds it took me to decide which way to turn three cars honked at me.

I found a gas station attendant, who directed me to a librarian (in a library) who showed me the computers. I marked down the address of the GPS, searched MapQuest for directions and scribbled them down on a tiny piece of paper with an even smaller pencil. I thanked the librarian on the way out and drove deeper into the city.

The farther I got into Manhattan, the less I liked driving. Cars stopped short in front of me, turned without signaling and honked non-stop. Which just confirmed my suspicions that I was not cut out to live in a city, and especially not *this* city.

I found parking in a high-rise lot a couple of blocks from where Hambecker had parked and made my way to the street. The sidewalk was crowded with people. They jostled by and I stepped back into a doorway. My plan had been to make my way to the parking lot where Hambecker was parked and see if I could figure out the most logical direction. Now that I was here I realized that was optimistic at best. I was surrounded by people and cars and buildings and there was no way I was going to figure out where he went.

I threaded my way into the stream of pedestrians skirting past the tables outside the restaurants. Passing Pellegrino's, I nearly stepped into traffic. Ledroit was sitting at a table with a man. At least, I thought it was Ledroit. Her face was different, hard. No sign of the grief she'd displayed at the office. I turned quickly and walked away, my heart beating. I crossed to the other side of the street and stopped behind an umbrella at Il Palazzo.

I watched them talk from across the street, Ledroit watchful, relaxed but ready. The man was talking fast, leaned forward, his hands moving in sync with his mouth.

He's afraid.

I shifted so I could see better, moving out from behind the umbrella just half a step, and I was grabbed at the bicep and dragged back toward a building and through a door. I brought my knee up as I turned, ready to attack, and stopped. I'd found Hambecker.

He was livid. The veins standing out at his temples face red, hands fisted.

"Are you trying to get yourself killed?" His voice was quiet, even and deadly.

"I was just—"

"Sticking your nose in things you don't understand." He closed his eyes and took a deep breath. When he opened them, he looked as angry as ever.

I began to feel afraid. Not that he'd hurt me, but that he might pop a gasket.

"That woman," I said, "is Michèle Ledroit," as he said, "Margaret LeDonne."

"What? Who did you say she is?" I asked.

"Margaret LeDonne. Very bad woman."

"But she told me her name is Michèle Ledroit. Her boyfriend Victor was in the white car." I wasn't thinking well. How could tearful Michèle Ledroit be ruthless Margaret LeDonne? "Who is the guy with her? Is that Victor Puccini?"

"He may be Victor Puccini here in New York, but he's Ronnie's brother, Hugh."

"You've seen him up close?" I asked. Hambecker couldn't be wrong, could he?

"Close enough. That's him." Hambecker looked out the glass front of the door.

I took a look around; we were in a narrow hall, mailboxes on the wall across from us, stairs to upper floors. A door labeled "office" was next to the mailboxes across from me.

Hambecker pulled his head back in the door. "They're still there. I don't want to risk LeDonne seeing you here, so we're going out the back.

"There doesn't appear to be a back. Just stairs up." I pointed to the dingy carpeted stairway. Not exactly welcoming.

"Then we'll go up." Hambecker grabbed my hand and towed me up the stairs.

I was distracted. In the past he'd grabbed my wrist or my arm. I couldn't remember him ever taking my hand before. I liked it. His hand was reassuring. Strong, dry and he wasn't holding me too tight. *A good hand.* Good Lord, I had to be losing my mind.

There was a window on the first landing and Hambecker dropped my hand to shove it open and stick his head out. He looked around and pulled it back in.

"We have to go up to the next floor and down to the other end," he said. He took my hand and we jogged up together. He pushed through the landing door and we turned left and headed to the end of the hall past a line of closed doors. It ended at a window, but Hambecker shook his head when he brought it back in.

"Can't get there from here either." He took my hand, and we jogged back down the hall to the stairs.

"Wait!" I said as he pulled open the door and started to send me through it. "Look, an elevator." We'd missed it before. It was recessed into the wall and we'd gone the other way.

We took the elevator to the roof. I didn't particularly *want* to go to the roof, but Hambecker insisted. He headed to the front of the building first, looking to see that LeDonne or Ledroit or whatever the heck her name turned out to be, was still there. She was speaking now, not that we could hear what she was saying but she was right in Victor's face and he didn't look happy.

He got up and started to back away from the table and I had a sudden and terrible vision of Ledroit pulling a gun and shooting him on the street. But she didn't. He moved away.

"Stay here," Hambecker said, moving fast across the roof. "I'll be right back."

I watched Victor move through the crowd and glanced back at Ledroit. She was talking to the waiter, not looking like she was going anywhere. I scanned for Victor. He'd moved further down the block than I'd anticipated, but he was still visible. Hambecker burst out onto the sidewalk and jogged in Victor's direction dodging people on the sidewalk. He must have got fed up because he left the sidewalk and was running against traffic in the street.

I held my breath as he weaved through the cars like he was in some action flick until he was on the other side of the road, approaching Victor. Then he had him and was pushing him through the crowd and down an alley. I lost sight of them and looked back to Ledroit. She had a take-out bag in her hand and was paying the waiter. Should I run down the stairs and follow her?

What had Hambecker said? Stay here? That was almost like a challenge for me to follow her. I got up and hurtled down the stairs. It was a lot of flights, I lost count at fourteen. Then I got a stitch in my side and had to slow down.

When I made street level and came out the door still holding my side, Ledroit was gone. I'd only seen the general direction she'd started out in. I dragged a chair from the restaurant out on the sidewalk and climbed on it, trying to catch sight of her. But a waiter ran out yelling at me in Italian so I had to get down. I hadn't seen her.

The question was, do I wait for Hambecker or just go back home? I hadn't even been in the city for an hour and I was already tired of it. I'd seen Victor, I'd seen Ledroit, and I'd seen them together. Which was dang interesting when I thought about it. Maybe I should go home before Hambecker found me and gave me another lecture.

I was sound asleep when I felt someone next to me on the bed and sat straight up and reached for the light.

"Easy, it's just me." He was a solid weight on the edge of my bed.

"Hambecker?" What was he doing at my house? I let the phone lay.

"Yeah. How many guys sneak into your house at night? Wait. I don't want to know that. Hang on, let me get a light." His weight shifted off the bed. There was a click and the hall light shone through my open door. He was in T-shirt and jeans—and stocking feet?

"Where are your shoes?" I asked.

"It's a lot easier to sneak around in sock feet. Also, my shoes were gross from a New York alley. I left them on your porch."

"I still don't get why my dogs don't bark at you." I pushed the pillows behind me and leaned against the headboard. "Did you talk to Victor? What did he say? How does he know Ledroit?" My brain was starting to kick in.

"Yes. We talked. It was very productive. But you didn't stay on the roof." He sat next to me on the edge of the bed. Very near.

"Ledroit—Donne, whatever, was on the move and I thought maybe I should follow her. Why are you here?" Not that I minded, what girl in her right mind would object to a handsome federal agent on her bed? But I did want to know how come he was on my bed.

"You disappeared, I wanted to check in, make sure you weren't any worse for wear. You didn't follow her, did you? That wouldn't be wise." He picked up my hand with both of his and rubbed my palm with his thumbs. Very distracting.

"No. She was gone by the time I got down the

stairs. I got a stitch in my side." And now I had a stitch in my brain. The electricity generated by his touch short-circuited my thought processes.

"Why didn't you take the elevator?" He was massaging my fingers one by one.

"I thought it would be faster to run down. You ran down, didn't you?" It was taking everything I had to focus on the conversation now.

"Something like that, only I didn't land on every step." He leaned in closer.

"Can you stop that?" I said. "I can't concentrate."

"I'll stop if you tell me how you knew where I was." He did stop, but he kept my hand.

"I might want to know where you are again sometime, and if I tell you, I won't be able to." I tried tugging but his fingers were circling my wrist. Not tight, not hurting me but like human handcuffs.

"Yes. That's what I'd like to avoid." He was very close, his eyes softer than I'd ever seen them and my breath caught in my throat.

"Is that why you came? To, um, question me?" Damn, my brain was shutting down.

"I came for this." He leaned in close his mouth centimeters from mine. His lips touched mine for a fraction of a second, the softest whisper of a kiss, and my mind went south. "Nice," Hambecker said his lips still far too close.

"What's nice?" Would it be rude to tell him to shut up and kiss me? *Probably.*

"Nice work tracking me down." He placed another feather-light kiss on my mouth.

"It was easy." This time the kiss was anything but light. I slid my arms around his neck as his tongue touched my lips. My brain was screaming, *Wait a minute!*

but my body said, *Oh, what the hell; I'm going to enjoy this while I can,* as I went under for the third time.

Hambecker broke the kiss and removed my arms gently from his neck.

"Did I do something wrong?" I asked.

"Hell, no. I just want to know how you managed to get into a locked vehicle." His lips were millimeters away from mine, where did he get the control to hold back?

I closed the distance and kissed him running my tongue across his lower lip. "I didn't break in. Didn't need to." I slid my arms around his neck again, pulling myself into his lap.

"Is it the antennae?" His tongue caressed my lip and I sank deeper.

"Nope. But if you stay the night I'll tell you in the morning."

He shifted me so he could kiss me below my ear. "Magnet?" he whispered.

"Duct tape." I wrapped my legs around his waist pressing the length of my torso against him. "I'm trying to seduce you. Concentrate."

"I am concentrating." He licked my neck and blew on it. "Bumper?" He breathed the word so quietly I barely hear it.

"Wheel well." I heard myself whisper it and it was too late to take it back. I pulled away. "You bastard, you did that on purpose."

"Yep." He grinned and kissed me lightly on the lips. "And now you can't follow me into trouble."

Hambecker looked sorry as he disengaged himself from me, but I was furious.

"You're going to take what you came for and leave, aren't you. I thought you'd stay if I told you." *Crap. I will not cry.*

"I know. I'm sorry. But I've got to go, and you can't come."

"Bastard. I thought you liked me." *I will not cry.*

"I do like you. And you know it. I like you so much that I don't want you dead." He moved into the hall and turned out the light.

"But you're leaving me. I thought you'd stay…" *Please stay.*

"Next time. Next time, I'll stay." He dropped a kiss on my head. "Next time." He was gone. Not once had my dogs barked.

When the engine noise of Hambecker's SUV died away, I let myself cry a little. But not too much, because it's hard to feel too sorry for yourself when the guy you like doesn't want you dead.

Chapter Ten

The phone started ringing before I was even out of bed the next day. If I could have answered it without opening my eyes, I would have. As it was, I only cracked them open enough to pick up the phone without knocking it over.

"Did you hear?" Meg. I should have known.

"Hear what? The phone ringing too damn early in the morning?" If she'd only hang up I could fade back into oblivion.

"Grant Fraser was found murdered in his bed last night. You've got to get that story."

"Grant?" Images started whirling around in my head. Grant at the bar surrounded by friends. Grant with his arm around me, talking to Hambecker. Grant in the RV at the racetrack, talking about being blackmailed. "Oh God."

"I've got to get you on a flight to Atlanta. We have to report this."

"I don't think you'll need to. I've got more information than I want at the moment. I'll talk to you later; I've got to call the cops."

I heard her say "What?" as I pressed the flash button.

I got Tom on the phone and before I could explain he said, "I know. Jim called. Come down and give a statement sometime today."

I hung up and dragged myself into the shower. My

thighs were killing me from stair climbing in New York City. The hot water helped until I used it up and then the cold water woke me up.

The phone rang again as I was getting dressed.

"Have you heard about Grant?" It was Claire this time. "What do you think happened?"

"I can't talk about it right now." I was hopping around, trying to pull on my jeans with one hand. "But I'll call you later."

Considering I knew more about it than the cops or Jim I thought I'd better keep my mouth shut until after I'd been to the barracks.

I fed the dogs and took the time to make myself a flat egg sandwich and wrapped it in a paper napkin to eat on the road. I poured coffee in a travel mug, called Max to ask him to feed the animals and do the barn chores. Ranger was sticking close, and I trusted his instincts, despite the fact he let Hambecker walk in whenever he wanted, so I loaded Ranger in the truck and took him with me.

I took a bite of sandwich and set it on the center console so I could pick up my coffee. When I went to pick it back up half of it was hanging out of Ranger's mouth.

"Hey, that's mine." I tore off the piece that hadn't been in his mouth and got another two bites of breakfast while Ranger wolfed the rest of it. "Dang Dog," I muttered and he leaned over and licked my face. Lovely.

When I got to the Barracks I dragged a towel out from behind the seat and wiped my face and hands. Then I unloaded Ranger and took him in the barracks with me. I could see the desk clerk debating if he should tell me the dog couldn't come in, but he just buzzed us through instead.

"You can't bring that horse in here," Tom said when we walked in his office. "He'll break something."

"He's having separation anxiety, I couldn't leave him." I sat in a chair and Ranger sat beside me. "He's my bodyguard."

"You need a bodyguard *why*?" Tom was kicked back in his chair looking at the ceiling. "I bet this is going to be good."

"Because I know more than anyone about Grant's death, and how it might tie in to the Bulgarian assassin in Planet Hair, and the Mob."

"You get knocked on the head or is this delusions of grandeur? Jim was at those races too. He didn't have anything to say about Bulgarian assassins." Tom sat up and leaned on his elbows. "So spill. What is it that you know that no one else seems to, and why do you know it?"

"Here goes…" I gave him my version of what happened in the RV at the races, then I reminded him about Ledriot asking me to find Victor Puccini. Lastly I told him about New York City. "… and so the woman I think of as Michèle Ledroit, Hambecker knows as Margaret LeDonne, who's supposed to be really dangerous and connected with the mob. Then there's the guy who is Ronnie's brother, she calls him Hughie. His name is Hugo Hart, I think, except it's also possible he's known by Victor Puccini. Also, Grant told us that the woman who blackmailed him had a French accent and was named Margaret."

"My God, I've got a headache. Two people with aliases? Two murders. A connection with the mob, and Bulgaria and assassins. I wish to hell you were pulling my leg, but you're not. How much of this does

145

Hambecker know?"

"More than me, probably. But not that Margaret threatened Grant, and he left to go somewhere secret last night so he may not know that Grant's been killed." My heart ached a little when we mentioned Grant's name. He'd been a hometown hero and a good guy. We'd miss him. "I assume Hambecker knows who Margaret really is and her connection to Hugo, and probably why the assassin was assassinated." I chuckled to myself. I was a laugh a minute, when I wasn't sobbing like a baby.

"I've got to get this information to the detective in Atlanta. Stick around and I'll have someone type this up for you to sign. I think Steve's at his desk if you want to terrorize him with Ranger while I'm on the phone to Atlanta."

I took the hint and Ranger and I strolled around to the bullpen to see what kind of trouble we could get Steve Leftsky into.

"Hey there, big boy," Steve said when we walked in. Ranger stuck his nose in Steve's lap and I pulled him away.

"Mind your manners, chowder head," I said.

"Yes, Ma'am," Steve responded.

"Not you, Leftsky, the dog." I sat in one of the rolling chairs and twirled around. Ranger looked bored and sat next to Steve, who was at least stationary.

When Tom came in with a statement for me to sign Ranger had his head in Steve's lap and I was researching Grant's death online. I could get the basic facts up on our website and do an in-depth article in next week's paper. An article I was uniquely qualified to write.

I signed, Ranger licked Steve in the ear, and we

headed to the truck. I'd decided to take Ranger to work with me.

Meg was pacing when I walked into the office with Ranger, balancing a cup of coffee and a walnut cinnamon roll.

"Finally," she said. "What took you so long?"

"You know paperwork." I dumped my bag and food on my desk and flopped in my chair. "What's going on here?"

"I want you to go to Atlanta and see what you can find out. This is huge." She sat on her desk and jumped off again almost immediately. "We need to run with the big dogs on this."

"Stop pacing. We'll do better than run with the big dogs. We'll lead them. I've got inside information and nothing I could find out in Atlanta would be news. It's all on the Internet already."

"I still think you should go to Atlanta. Tom can call the captain there and get you access." Meg was walking the floor, talking with her hands and just generally exuding nervous energy.

"Calm down. I think Grant's death is tied into the Bulgarian assassin in Planet Hair. What's his name Albert, Alvin—I've got it written down on my desk." I searched through a stack of notes. "Albin. Albin Shvakova. If that's true, this is a bigger story than anyone knows. Anyone except you, me, Hambecker and Tom."

"And whoever killed them," Meg said. "That person obviously knows." She stopped pacing and sat. "Not to change the subject, but do you think we should have Ronnie clean here? Everyone says she's a wiz."

"And she probably could use the money. That house she lives in is pretty run down." I grabbed a legal pad from the shelf behind Deirdre's desk and sat at my desk.

"Shouldn't you be out finding the murderer or something?" Meg said. "Or do you think he'll just waltz in here and tell you his story?"

"He's a she. And no probably not, but I'm making an effort not to blindly dive in and get taken by surprise. Looking at the connections. Figuring out my next step."

"Don't spend too much time figuring, you do your best work when you blindly dive in. You've got a knack for stepping right in the middle of stuff."

"Hmm." I may have a knack for stepping into stuff, but I'd rather develop some caution and maybe step next to situations rather than right into the middle of them. So I wrote a time-line.

Body in Planet Hair
Find Car
Murder suspects Ronnie's brother (I didn't seriously think Ronnie had the ability to kill someone.) Lori (unlikely), Jim (probably not even though it would be poetic justice and a hell of a story), Claire (highly unlikely.)
Ledroit shows up looking for Victor Puccini (I've never heard of him)
Hambecker arrives
Hugo Hart is mixed up with the mob (Ronnie's brother)
There was a bullet in the wall at Planet Hair

The dead guy's name is Albin Shvakova and he's a Bulgarian hit man.

Grant was threatened by a woman named Margaret. (French)

Hambecker follows Hugo to NYC. Hugo meets with Michèle.

Hambecker calls Michèle Margaret
Is Hugo really Victor Puccini?
Grant is murdered
Does Hambecker know why Shvakova was in the country?

The first thing I needed to find out was if my hunch about Victor was right. Was he also known as Victor Puccini? I picked up my bag, looked around for my pastry and realized it was gone. Had I eaten it without noticing? Ranger was licking his chops.

"You ate my breakfast, didn't you?" I shook my finger at him.

"What are you talking about?" Meg asked.

"Ranger ate my bun, that's all." I gave him the evil eye.

"Nothing unusual about that. Are you going now?"

"Yep, I'm out of here. Come on, Ranger."

I debated taking Ranger home before I drove out to Ronnie's, but it was a cool enough day, and Ronnie didn't have any dogs he would upset, so I drove straight up Route 110. I was happy to see the pickup was behind the shed when I pulled into the drive. I wanted to talk to Hugo.

"Hi Bree!" Ronnie was already out on the porch when I got out of my truck, leaving the windows cracked so Ranger wouldn't get too hot, or run out of oxygen, but not so open he could jump out and terrorize Ronnie. I waved hello and walked over to sit on the porch step next her.

She was watching Ranger sniff the air through the open window.

"He can't get out," I said. "He wouldn't hurt you if he could. He's big, but he's gentle."

"I'm not afraid. Can I pet him?" She looked at me her eyes wide, smiling with no reservation. She acted with such innocent happiness; I didn't think I'd ever get used to that much guilelessness in an adult face.

"Sure, you can pet him if you want."

We walked over to the truck and I let Ranger out and asked him to sit and stay. I didn't want Ronnie to get knocked over by accident and start to fear big dogs. He put up with her handling with good grace and licked her hands and face. She laughed and called him a good boy. She looked so happy that it hurt me. I didn't know what she'd gotten in the middle of, but whatever it was not only wasn't she to blame, she also wasn't responsible. Even so, her life was going to be changed. Her brother's association with the mob wasn't going to leave her untouched. I blinked back the unexpected tears and put Ranger back in the truck.

"Can I see him again sometime?" Ronnie asked her eyes bright with dog infatuation.

"Of course, anytime," I said. Not knowing if there'd be a next time at all. "Do you live here alone, Ronnie?

"Yep. I know how to cook and shop and drive. Hughie taught me. I never go on the freeway. He said that would be bad." She took my hand, and quickly dropped it. "Hughie told me that grownups don't hold hands. But I forget sometimes."

"Does Hugo visit you often?" I couldn't bring myself to call him Hughie.

150

"Almost every week." She had a big smile now. "He's here now. Hughie has been visiting me. He's on vacation." She opened the door to the kitchen and led me in. "Hughie, somebody's here!"

The basement door opened and a short sandy haired man stepped into the kitchen. His face was tense and there were bags under his eyes. "Ronnie, go upstairs and sweep the carpet. I need to talk to Bree."

"Okay, Hughie." Ronnie ran down the hall and I moment later I heard the low hum of the vacuum cleaner.

"You're that reporter who came here with the fed." There wasn't an ounce of welcome in his voice and his face was like granite.

"Bree MacGowan." I stuck out my hand. He didn't hesitate, which surprised me; he took my hand in a firm, dry grip that didn't hurt, and didn't last too long. He may be a crook, but he had manners.

"Sit down, Ms. MacGowan." He pulled out a chair for me, and took the one opposite, facing the door. I was not surprised.

"Call me Bree," I said. "But I'm not sure what to call you. Ronnie calls you Hugh, but I'm almost certain you're the man Michèle Ledroit is looking for, Victor Puccini."

"My full name is Victor Hugo Puccini." A slight smile softened his face. "My mother had a sense of humor. Ronnie never liked Victor; it was too full of hard sounds when she was little. She's always called me Hugh."

"You're her brother from different fathers?" I hazarded a guess.

"Yeah, that's not unusual is it?" He raised his brows at me.

"No," I smiled. Considering the MacGowan habit of not marrying at all, I couldn't pass judgment. "You take care of Ronnie."

"I've tried. But truthfully, things have gotten out of hand and I need help. I'm willing to make a deal with the cops if it means Ronnie will be safe, but I'm not talking until I have proof. And it's not going to be easy, because she's not entirely innocent. If I wasn't desperate I wouldn't talk, but it won't be long now until Margaret finds me, and when she does she will hurt Ronnie in ways Ronnie wouldn't be able to recover from. I can't let that happen."

"Why didn't she take you out at the restaurant the other day?"

He looked at me sharply. "Did Hambecker tell you about that?"

"No. I was there. I saw you." I didn't see the harm in offering him the truth as a gesture of good faith.

"You followed me?" He looked slightly shocked. "I didn't realize you knew I was here. I must be slipping."

"Actually, I followed Hambecker. He was following you. I didn't put Hugo together with Victor until I saw you with Michèle Ledroit. That was Michèle, wasn't it? She doesn't have a twin?"

"Her name is Margaret 'Widow-Maker' LeDonne, and she is the Consigliore for Shirley 'The Shredder' Gambino. They are not people you should get messed up with." His voice was tinged with regret.

"But then why did she introduce herself as Michèle? Why come to me at all?" I would have been mortified except this story was going to be all mine. And it was big.

"She uses Michèle Ledroit when she doesn't want her identity to be discovered. Even the Widow-Maker

CRAZY LITTLE THING CALLED DEAD

cannot kill everyone whose services she uses. She needed a local, someone who would notice a stranger. That's why you. If she ever finds out how much you know, you'll be dead."

"In other words, after I write this story my life will be in danger. I'll be screwed." *Well, shit.*

"Pretty much." He pitied me.

"Why should I help you then? If I'm going to have to choose between telling the story and my life?" *Damn, damn, damn.* I would tell this story.

"You could write under an assumed name."

"That wouldn't save me. But truthfully, I'm tired of this game. I'll help you because Ronnie needs help. She doesn't need to be alone in this world. Tell me why she's in danger." *Forget ramifications and cut to the chase already, MacGowan. There's nothing to be done for it.*

"Bring me written proof that Ronnie will be safe, signed by someone who can make it happen and I'll give you the story. God help you if you run it." He stood up and offered me his hand. I thought he was going to help me up, but he shook mine. As if to seal the deal.

"Hambecker is out of town, and I don't know when he'll be back, but as soon as he is, we'll work this out. I'm assuming the state police won't be able to give you what you want."

"Wait for Hambecker. He has a stake in this. He'll be willing to make it happen."

He showed me out, the drone of the vacuum still emanating from the upper floors. I wondered how long Ronnie would continue to clean before her brother stopped her.

I stopped in at the Brain Freeze for a chocolate cone with the works on the way back to the office. I made Ranger lie down with his head facing his door so I could eat it, and he kept shooting me dirty looks over his shoulder. Driving while eating a cone is dicey, add a dog's butt in your lap and it becomes ridiculous. Every so often he'd wag his tail and smack me in the face. There was dog hair in my chocolate.

"You turkey."

I tried pinning his tail under my other arm, but it just didn't work. I almost gave him the rest of the dog-covered cone then I remembered that dogs can't eat chocolate. So I ate it anyway, hair and all.

Hugo had confirmed two of my assumptions; Margaret and Michèle were one and the same, as were Victor Puccini and Hugo Hart. The size of the other team had just been halved. I didn't much like what I'd heard of LeDonne, but Victor/Hugo seemed decent enough. I wondered how he'd gotten mixed up with the mafia.

Meg laughed when I walked in the door.

"What?" I asked, but I figured I must have ice cream on my face.

"Go look in the mirror," she said. "You look like you're about four years old."

Sure enough I had chocolate and dog hair on my face and shirt to feed a small army. It took me a minute to figure out that when Ranger's tail had gotten hair on my ice cream he'd also gotten ice cream on his tail. Which he'd wagged all over me. I vowed never to eat ice cream with Ranger in the car again and cleaned myself up.

The tough part was now that I had something concrete, I couldn't do anything about it. Until Hambecker re-appeared, I was stuck. And I wanted the story before the next *Star* came out. For one brief moment I considered interviewing Ledroit, but self-preservation put the kibosh on that pretty quick. I wasn't ready to get dead. I made Tom promise to call me if Hambecker was back in town and settled down to wait.

I wasn't good at waiting. I made a batch of brownies and ate them all. Not good. Thursday evening was spent lying on my bed groaning, and not in a good way.

The funeral was Friday afternoon. I dressed as appropriately as I knew how, which in this case was a black swirly skirt, and black and red peasant blouse and my slouchy cowboy boots. No way was I walking through a cemetery in high heels. Parking was tight around the green. I should have thought to ride the Kawasaki, although the Kawasaki was not so compatible with the skirt. I snagged a spot near Planet Hair and walked across the Green to the church with the red door.

The place was packed and hushed. Muffled weeping accompanied me up the aisle toward the front, where I squeezed in next to Claire. "Nice duds," she whispered. If circumstances were different I would have laughed, she wore a classy black suit which I was sure was designer, and black leather pumps with a pretty, but sensible-for-cemeteries, heel.

When the minister started to speak the entire front pew began to sob. Men and women both held tissues and handkerchiefs to stricken faces. I held my body still trying to still my own urge to break down. Claire grabbed my hand and squeezed it. I squeezed back. We were both bawling by the time the service was over and friends and family had all spoken. My heart was breaking for Grant's family, for the community's loss and for the man who had so casually held me close while he chatted with Hambecker. Underneath the sorrow was a growing fury at Margaret LeDonne.

Claire and I stood together at the gravesite while the minister said a few words and lowered the casket into the ground. We threw in flowers and racing confetti of minute checkered flags and little golden trophies. I didn't even know him that well and I wanted to throw myself on the grass and sob. I couldn't imagine how his sisters were feeling.

As Claire and I walked toward the road I caught the glimpse of stylish black hair and froze. My heart was step dancing in my chest.

"What?" Claire caught the direction of my gaze and started craning her neck. "What do you see?"

"Stop. Don't look. I think it's the woman who threatened to kill Grant. She's got some nerve being here. Go on back to your car; I've got to tell Tom."

"I'm coming with you." Claire grabbed my arm. "I want to see her."

"No. No you don't. People who see her die. Please, Claire. I can't take another murder right now." I could see that she wanted to object, but whatever it was she saw in my face stopped.

She nodded. "I'll see you there. Stay safe."

I found Tom standing in a group of troopers and their families. I placed my hand on his arm and drew him away. I had spotted the black haired woman and caught a look at her face. It was Ledroit.

"Michèle Ledroit is here," I said. "The woman who threatened Grant."

"Where?" He asked. "But don't point."

As if I would.

"On the street next to the big maple. Across from Garret Flint's angel." She was standing her back to a sleek Mercedes, surveying the mourners. I don't think she'd spotted me; the cemetery was pretty full of people.

"I'll take care of this. Get in your car and go to the wake. Do not—and I mean it, Bree—do *not* go anywhere alone. Got that?" Tom was watching me carefully, probably looking for signs of rebellion.

"Yeah, I've got it." And I probably would have obeyed the command if my car hadn't been in her direction. The closer I got to where she was standing, the madder I got and the faster I walked. I was close enough that she would have heard if I'd called her name, but she was looking the other way and my plan was to take her out at the knees and choke the life out of her. I was one car length away and I broke into a jog, putting a little power behind my tackle when I was grabbed around the waist from behind and whisked around the back of a truck.

"What—" I began.

"Shh! Lower your voice. Are you trying to get yourself killed?" Hambecker let me go and I whirled on him.

"Why'd you stop me," I hissed. "I had her. She was mine."

"It can't happen like that. I'm sorry. I know it's hard to let her walk free. But if you grab her now we can't charge her with anything. We have no proof." His hand was around my wrist, restraining but not hurting me.

"Charge her? I was going to kill her." I was tugging now, struggling. My heart hadn't stopped its furious beating. I could still get her.

Chapter Eleven

"You'd be dead before Tom had time to arrest you. No. Come on. Leave your truck here; I'm taking you to the wake." Hambecker steered me across the grass, away from the place Ledroit stood unmolested by me, to where his Escalade was parked. I wasn't in the car two minutes before the unused adrenaline in my body backed up on me and I burst into tears. Hambecker gathered me in his arms and held me close, which just upset me more. I didn't want him to see me cry.

"Easy now," He said. "It's going to be all right."

"I'm not crying," I sobbed. "I'm mad."

"I know, you're frustrated. I stopped you from taking charge. You can hit me if you want." He had me tight. I couldn't have hit him if I'd wanted to.

"She killed Grant. He was so alive, and she killed him. I hate her." I was calming down, the sobs weren't as uncontrollable. I let Hambecker hold me a couple of minutes longer so he'd feel like he was doing something. "I'm okay now," I said. I pulled away and dragged a tissue from my pocket. "We can go to the party."

"Wake," he said, snapping on his seatbelt and putting the key in the ignition. "It's not a party, it's a wake. There's a difference."

"How's it different?" I pulled down the visor to inspect the damage. Red nose, red eyes, smeared mascara. Great.

159

"There's a lot more drinking at a wake than a party."

"I'd forgotten that. It's a good thing I'm not driving." Victor Hugo Puccini popped into my head. "Hey, I've got something to tell you—I talked to Hugh, Ronnie's brother." I could see the lecture forming in his brain. "He wants a deal. If you can promise him Ronnie will be protected, he'll turn state's evidence." I looked at him expectantly. "That's good, isn't it?"

"Yes. That is very good. When I talked to him Wednesday it didn't seem like he'd turn." He drummed on the steering wheel. "This will move things along." He parked the car at the little senior center that was being used as the reception hall.

I unbuckled and he reached across the SUV and pulled me to him. "Thanks." He dropped a kiss on my head and let me go, which had the unfortunate effect of reminding me of the other night. I was mad when he opened the car door. He stepped back warily, and eyed me.

"What just happened?" he asked. "Did I miss something?"

"Tuesday night. You kissed me just like that before you disappeared for two days."

"Is there any point in saying I'm sorry?" His face was so much like a little boy, his eyes big and eyebrows raised and a tentative smile that I didn't blast him the way I'd planned.

"You are such a child. Come on, we're missing the toasts."

There was a familiar Mercedes SUV parked in front of my house when I arrived home, and the dogs raising holy hell in the house. As I slid out of my truck the driver door of the SUV opened and Michèle Ledroit got out. Crap. Really, really bad timing. I should have stayed and got drunk at the wake with the rest of the town.

"You found my house." My heart was beating hard. I wiped my hands on my jeans.

"Not difficult. You are well known and your neighbors are quite obliging." She had her purse over her shoulder and a large manila envelope in her hand.

"Hard not to be well known in a town this size." I'd left my purse in my truck so I had exactly nothing in my hands. I felt naked. "Why are you here? I would have called if I'd had any information."

"I assumed you'd call me if you found Victor Puccini." She opened the envelope and I got a very bad feeling in the pit of my stomach. The crying girlfriend has gone. This was the Margaret LeDonne I'd seen on the street in New York.

"I didn't find him." I was finding it hard to breathe right.

"See this?" She pulled a photo from the envelope. "This is a photo of you. In New York City, across the street from where I was speaking with Victor Puccini."

It was a picture of Hambecker and me taken through the glass door of the building we'd been hiding in. We were arguing. My blood turned to ice. Did she know who Hambecker was? I felt like the mice Annabelle Cat played catch and release with in the field. Any moment could be my last, or Michèle could get tired of tracking me and I could go free.

161

"I was having dinner with a friend in the city. I had no idea Victor was there." I willed the panic back down into the recesses of my mind. I needed to think.

"My instincts tell me you're hiding something from me, and my instincts are rarely wrong." She pulled a small handgun from her bag. "Perhaps a little target practice? That lovely cat on the porch rail?" She pulled the trigger and Annabelle the cat squealed and jumped. She was around the house in a flash. I went to the porch, no blood.

"Tell me." Another shot rang out, one of the small rectangles of glass in my door shattered and there was a yelp from in the house. Breathing was nearly impossible.

"Stop shooting. I'll tell you. He's at his sister's house in Chelsea. You couldn't find her because she has a different last name. But that's where he is. Her name is Carly Simons." I gave her the address of the courthouse in Chelsea, hoping she wouldn't think to Google it before she left.

"If you are not telling the truth, every last one of those animals will die. And then so will you."

Ledroit/LeDonne got into her car and drove away, leaving me shattered on the porch.

I ran inside. Ranger was under the table whimpering. There was blood on his shoulder, staining his grey coat. I crawled under the table and put my hand on his head. "Easy boy. Easy now." His shoulder was a mess. "Come on baby. Let's go."

He crawled out from under the table and cried out as he stood. Fresh blood oozed onto his shoulder. I knew I should pack it, but time was short. He limped out to the truck with me and I helped him in. I was dialing as I backed around and headed out. First, the vet, who agreed to stay open until I got there. Then Tom. Not at the office. I tried home. The line was busy. I tried the number Victor gave me.

"Listen," I said when he answered. "You don't have much time. Ledroit—LeDonne, whatever her name is, knows you are in town. I sent her to Chelsea, but it won't be long before she figures out that's wrong and comes after you. Get Ronnie out of there." I hung up. I didn't have time to commiserate.

I tried the house again and this time got Tom.

"Meet me at the animal hospital. Ledroit is back in town. She shot Ranger. She might have got Annabelle too, but I didn't have time to go looking." I drove as safely as I could with Ranger bleeding in the seat beside me.

The whole crew was still in the office when I got to the animal hospital, which surprised me. I was after four on a Friday afternoon.

The vet tech took Ranger from me as I walked in, saying "She scrubbing up in the back, do you want to come with him?"

"Normally I would, you know that. But the state police are meeting me. He's in good hands." I rubbed Ranger behind the ears. "Good boy," I said quietly, "you go on back."

Tom drove up before I had time to sit down in the waiting area and I went out to meet him. He unlocked the passenger side of his cruiser and I got in. I'd been in emergency mind-set. Doing triage in my mind, Ranger first, then the people, praying I'd find Annabelle Cat safe when I got home. Knowing that I'd be in hot trouble when Ledroit found out I'd sent her on a wild goose chase. I took a deep breath and steadied myself. It wouldn't do me any good to fall apart now.

"Just relax for a minute, Richard is joining us. You look like you could use a break." Tom was frowning at me but I couldn't be bothered to figure out why. I was busy trying to stem the rising panic. Maybe two minutes went by before I heard a vehicle pull in next to us. The rear door opened and Hambecker slid into the back.

"So MacGowan, is blood the new black or what?" His voice was tight.

"What are you talking about?" I pulled down the visor and flipped open the mirror. I was a bloody mess. "Ranger got shot. It must be his blood. Just deal with it."

"That explains why we're meeting at the animal hospital. Is he going to be okay?" Hambecker was very matter of fact, which was calming.

"I think so. There's a lot of blood, but I don't think the wound is very deep." I sighed. "We don't have time to worry about Ranger right now. Michèle Ledroit, ugh, Margaret LeDonne, whatever her name is—"

"Let's just agree to call her Ledroit, it will be simpler for you," Tom said.

"I sent her on a wild goose chase to Chelsea, but she's going to be coming after me and Victor, both. She has a picture of us in New York, Hammie. In the foyer of that building. She doesn't seem to know who you are, but she knew that I knew who Victor was. I called Victor and told him to get lost."

To Hambecker's credit he swore softly under his breath but didn't yell at me for screwing up his case. "The question is," he said, "what do we do now? We've got a case against LeDo—Ledroit but we need Puccini to prosecute. We can't offer him protection if we can't find him. We need to keep you out of Ledroit's way."

"I'm going to radio the Sherriff office in Chelsea.

I'll tell them to keep an eye out for Ledroit and detain her for the slightest infraction. Hopefully she'll be pissed off enough to do something stupid and we'll be able to keep her off the streets for a couple of days." Tom got on the radio and got cooperation from the sheriff. "Hopefully we can catch a break there. Next thing is, how do we keep you safe? I guess we could lock you in a holding cell at the barracks."

"Oh, joy. Just what I've always wanted." Although, if I were to be truthful, lockup sounded way better than dead.

"No need," Hambecker said. "I'll keep her with me. If we don't get lucky in Chelsea I'll take her to a hotel. If we *do* get lucky and Ledroit is stuck in lockup for a couple of days, I'll stay at her place."

"If I have to go to a hotel I'm taking the dogs with me. I'm not leaving them to be picked off one at a time by Ledroit." In the course of the conversation, I'd transformed from terrified to raging anger. That bitch shot my dog.

My veterinarian came out of the building and beckoned to me. I got out of the car and went to her. I noticed that both Tom and Hambecker got out too. It seemed I'd gained two bodyguards.

"He's fine," the doctor said. "The bullet grazed him and he bled some, but we've stitched him up. He'll be sore for a couple of days. You can take him home."

I burst into tears.

Hambecker and I left my truck at the animal hospital and were on our way to Ronnie's when we got some good news. The Chelsea sheriff discovered Michèle Ledroit swearing in front of the courthouse. When he went to detain her she round-housed him with her purse. The purse had her gun in it, which wouldn't have been a problem—it's not illegal to carry concealed weapons in Vermont—but the impact made the Deputy see stars and he charged her with assault on a police officer. We'd gotten a reprieve.

The mood in the SUV lightened considerably, and I felt the knot in my chest ease as we drove the rest of the way up Route 110. Ranger would be okay, Annabelle Cat would come home and Ledroit would be confined to the Chelsea jailhouse for at least a couple of day. You could almost call me cheerful.

Neither Ronnie nor her brother were at the house, not that I was surprised. If it were me, I'd be long gone. Hambecker took a jog around the property but there was no sign of them. We climbed back into the Escalade and he pulled back onto the road, headed toward home and relaxed in the glow of oncoming lights.

We slowed as we came to an old stone railroad crossing bridge. The opening under it was low and narrow, allowing only one car at a time to pass under. We started to pull through, but something was wrong. Headlights illuminated the interior of the Escalade as a car on the other side headed straight for us.

"Fuck!" In a split second Hambecker accelerated out from under the bridge and turned sharply left. I sucked in my breath and held it so I wouldn't scream like a little girl. The headlights raked me and then I was clear, but the other car caught the rear panel and the noise was horrific. The force of the impact spun us into the other vehicle and my head hit the window.

My brain exploded into little points of blinding light and pain. My vision was all bouncing dots of flash and shadow. I blinked and wiped blood from my face, checking on Hambecker, but his door was open and his seat was empty. How'd he get out of the car so fast?

I felt in my pocket for my cell phone and punched 911. Dispatch told me help was on the way and to stay on the line, but I needed air. I fumbled with the seatbelt buckle and the door handled. I really didn't want to be sick in Hambecker's SUV. I got the door open but misjudged the distance to the ground and fell. The cooler air helped and I decided not to throw up after all.

I pulled myself up the open door until I was standing. The world was unstable around me, so I held on, trying to think of what to do. 911 was coming. But where was Hambecker? I used the hood to steady myself and stumbled around the front of the vehicle to the driver side. Hambecker wasn't anywhere to be seen.

I imagined I could already hear sirens, that couldn't be right, could it? But they definitely were getting louder. The Barracks wasn't so far away; the State Troopers would get here first. I started to circle the SUV, leaning on any part that would hold me. As I came around the back I saw sunglasses that might be Hambecker's, but as I started toward them someone grabbed my arm. I jerked away, but that made me stumble and there was more pain as my head hit the back of the car, and I fell to the ground. I hit the ground hard and the blacktop hurt like hell. Waves of darkness washed over me, and I wanted to fight them, to find Hambecker, but my head hurt too much to focus.

I woke up in a basic basement room: cement halfway up the walls; unfinished ceiling; bare bulb hanging. Hambecker was face down on the mattress next to me. I tried to sit up and heard the door close across the room. The lock slid. It took me a minute to focus, but when I did, Victor was sliding the key into his pocket.

The sour smell of mildew permeated the room. There was some light coming in from the two small windows on the south wall, but the bulb overhead was broken. I knelt next to Hambecker. His face was turned toward me but his eyes were at half-mast. He looked at me with some recognition but then his eyes closed. I reached for his wrist to check his pulse as Victor came up beside me. I ignored him, counting beats.

"Where are we?" I asked, when I was sure Hambecker's heartbeat was steady.

"Ronnie's house. We were going to take you to Canada, but he told me Margaret was cooling her heels for a few days, so we brought you back here." He was holding something, hiding it with his hands.

"How could Hambecker tell you anything? He's out cold." I tapped his face again.

"He wasn't sedated then." Whatever it was he had in his hands, it had his full attention.

I turned back to Hambecker. "Is he okay? What did you give him?"

"Doesn't matter, he'll come out of it in a while."

I looked up and saw that he had a set of cuffs open in his hands. Before I could react he'd snapped one side onto my left wrist. I opened my mouth to protest and he clicked the other onto Hambecker's wrist.

"What the hell?"

"Sorry," he shrugged, "I need to keep tabs on the two of you, it's easier if you're both in one place."

"Let me go, you ass. I can't help him if we're handcuffed together."

"He's fine. It won't be for long. Just until I get everything straightened out." He was backing away from me, slipping the keys into his pocket. "I'll be back later." He locked the door behind him.

"Shit! Hambecker, wake up!" I slapped him on the face with the flat of my hand. His eyelids twitched but he didn't wake up. I looked around the room. Cement floor. The wall with the door was normal; the other three were cement half way up. There were two windows high on the wall, but they were too small for me to fit through, forget Hambecker.

In one corner, there were paint cans piled with a tarp and brushes. I moved as far from the bed as I could without rolling Hambecker onto the floor. This meant I could get five feet from the bed at most. I looked at him. He still unconscious, but he wouldn't thank me for sitting around, waiting for him to wake up. I grabbed his wrist with both of my hands and pulled. He was unmovable.

"Shit."

I grabbed his far wrist and tugged. He rolled toward me, and off the bed onto the floor, only now the arm with the handcuff was trapped under his body so I was jerked to the floor as well. I uttered some choice words and struggled to roll him back over again.

By the time he was back on his back, his cuffed hand out from under him, I was sweating and swearing. I still had to get him over to the tools, and then back across the room again. If I remembered Ronnie's basement correctly, the room next to this one contained the bulkhead door that opened to the outside. If I could get us through the wall we could get free.

The problem was getting him across the room. I stretched his arm as far as I could and then lay on the floor, sliding my feet in the direction of the stuff I needed. I was still a good five feet short. "Fuck." I climbed over Hambecker, set my back against the bed and shoved him in the gut with my feet. I wiped the sweat from my face with my free arm and tried again. He rolled over onto his stomach. I pushed his side with my feet until I'd stretched my arm to its limit. There were footsteps on the stair, and there was nothing I could do to hide my attempts to move across the room.

The door opened and Victor walked in on us. He laughed when he saw me sitting on the floor. "Getting your exercise?" He pointed to a bruise on Hambecker's head. "He's not going to be happy with you when he wakes up." He put a tray of food down near the bed and grabbed Hambecker under the armpits and lifted him back onto the bed, pulling me along with him. Then he picked up the tray and put it on the bed.

"Eat. You'll need your strength if you're going to be pulling him around the room with you."

I looked at the food and back at Hambecker. "Thanks." I'd starve before I touched anything Victor was offering.

He stood there, waiting. I picked up the fork and stuck it in a French fry. "You know, I have a really hard time eating when people are watching me," I said. This from the woman who'd eat anything, anywhere. Victor nodded and got up. "My sister is like that too. I'll come back later."

And I'll be gone.

I started the whole process over again. Rolling Hambecker off the bed onto the floor, he was going to develop stacking goose eggs. Only this time, when I braced my back against the bed and started to shove, he groaned. I shoved again, he groaned some more. Thank God.

"Wake up."

"I am awake. What happened?" He went to touch his forehead with his left hand and my arm went with him, nearly upsetting my balance. Just what I needed, to be using Hambecker for a pillow.

"Watch it. We're connected at the wrist."

"I see that." He was looking at the cuffs. "What's the deal?

"We are in the basement at Ronnie's house. I don't know how long you've been here, but I joined you less than an hour ago. Victor handcuffed me to you immediately, so mostly I've been pushing you around the room. Just when I was almost at the tools he came back and put you back on the bed. I had to start over again."

He rubbed his forehead with his free hand. "You do this?"

"Sorry. There was no gentle way to get you off the bed."

He sat up. "Hmm. Wow. Whatever he hit me with was strong. What day is it?"

"It's still today. You don't happen to have handcuff keys in your pocket?"

Hambecker rummaged in his pockets. He went to

put his left hand in his pocket and my hand went with him. He smiled. "This has some interesting possibilities."

"Right. Grow up." My face flushed hot, damn it.

"No keys," he said. "What's your plan for getting out of here?"

"The bulkhead door is in the next room. I didn't get a chance to check the door, but I know it's locked and there's also a padlock on the outside. Wallboard, I've had some experience with. It wouldn't take long to bust through into the next room, and it would be quieter than busting down the door."

"Decent plan. Windows?"

"Too small for either of us to crawl through."

"Do I smell food?"

"Yeah. It's on the bed. But I wouldn't eat it, if I were you. It's probably drugged."

"True. I'm going to stand up now."

We stood up in tandem, and I steadied him. His face turned pale and he broke out in a sweat, and I panicked. If he lost his cookies, I was going to lose my lunch. I don't have a positive history with vomit.

"I'm ready to move."

I kept an eye on him as we crossed the room. If he fell from standing he might be knocked out cold again. There was a blue tool among the paintbrushes and stir sticks. I snatched it up and pulled Hambecker to the other side of the room. I didn't even offer to let him do the job, I just took the tool in my left, unshackled hand and thunked the wall a couple of times creating a hole.

I stopped to listen, but it was quiet on the stairs. I set the tool on the cement ledge and started prying the wall with my fingers. My fingers weren't really strong enough; it was an inefficient way to take down the wall.

I picked up the tool again and used it to demolish the edges of the hole, making it bigger.

Hambecker must have regained his wits. "Here, let me," he said, and with both hands, my wrist dangling from his, he levered huge chunks away until the sixteen inches between the studs was clear. Now we just had to get through the sheetrock on the other side. The lower, cement, part of the wall stood about four feet high. I grabbed the blue tool and prepared to whack the heck out of the other side.

"Stop. There's an easier way. I just have to figure it out factoring in the handcuffs." He looked around the room, taking in the paint can piles and the bed. "Not much here. Help me move the bed."

Moving the bed turned out to be harder than anticipated. For one thing, we couldn't stand at either end and lift. Not that I could have lifted it anyway, the wooden frame weighed a ton. We used our combined weight, and Hambecker's leg strength (I knew rock hard thighs had to be handy for something), and pushed with our backs to the headboard. It moved a few inches, and the whole time I was waiting for Victor to come down the stairs and figure out what we were doing.

We stopped when the foot of the bed was about three feet from the hole we'd made, which confused me. But I followed Hambecker's lead, not that I had a choice, and went to stand next to him at the footboard.

"This is going to be tricky; because I'm not sure I can control the landing on the other side. I want you on the bed. I'm going to launch myself through the wall, feet first. That should take most of the wall out and I'll try to land on my feet. But you'll still have to follow me through, so when I yell 'now' I want you to use the mattress as a spring board and dive after me. You'll have to twist and go through sideways or you won't fit."

Whatever Victor gave him must have addled his brains. "Are you nuts? You may be trained to perform circus acts, but I'm not. Can't we just break through the wall with the blue tool and then crawl through? It seems so much easier."

"Easier is not always better. This will be faster."

"I don't have the skills for this Hambecker."

"You don't need skills, but fine. I'll kick out the wall and then go through easy." He set both hands on the end of the bed, raised himself up onto his arms so that his back was straight and his feet were flat on the wall. He kicked hard with both feet and the wall popped off and fell to the floor, then he lowered himself back to the floor. "Get off the bed and come stand next to me."

Chapter Twelve

I did as I was told, and stood next to him. He repeated his handstand, but this time he lowered his legs through the opening, twisting his body so that his hips and shoulders would fit through, and at the last minute pushed off so that his body shot through the hole in a controlled fall. He grasped the cement wall so I wasn't yanked through the wall after him. That would have hurt.

"What do I do?"

"Come here." He grabbed me under my arms and lifted, which was awkward in the extreme, partially because my left arm was by necessity wrapped across my chest, and partially because his arms were pressed against my breasts. He stopped lifting when my feet were just free of the ground and grinned.

"More interesting possibilities." He leaned in, and my heart started hammering as he rested his shoulders on the wall studs and lifted me higher. I got my knees onto the ledge and Hambecker twisted my shoulders to slide me through the opening. My foot caught and I wiggled it free, my legs popped loose and I body slammed Hambecker with my lower half. It was like hitting a brick wall.

We turned to leave and that's when the left hand cuffed to left hand situation really got awkward. He started forward and about yanked my arm out of the socket. "Hey!" I said, and yanked back, which put his hand level with my groin. Not good. Finally I fell in behind him, matching his stride. When he went to open the bulkhead door he pushed with both hands which yanked me up against his back.

"Watch it."

"I like this. You're kind of like a puppet."

"Puppet my ass."

"No, puppet *my* ass." I could hear the grin in his voice. It was highly irritating. I followed him out into the heat, around the house and up onto the porch, my hair sticking to my forehead and the back of my neck. He stopped next to the door, tight against the wall.

"I know this is not in your skill set, but we need to be as quiet as possible."

"We're not going in the house? Can't we just leave?"

"If getting out of here was the priority, that's what I'd be doing. Follow me." His shoulders shook with silent laughter.

"Jackass," I said. Having no choice, I parroted his steps. We crept through the cool kitchen stopping to check the living room. Victor wasn't on the first floor. Hambecker led me up the stairs, and when he stopped three quarters of the way up my face made contact with his back. I couldn't believe he smelled so fresh. Like soap even. I smelled like sweat, disgusting. Life was not fair.

We crept through the upstairs, listening at doors and edging them open as silently as only Hambecker could. We reached the room where I'd seen signs of habitation, mattress on the floor, clothes scattered, and I tensed expecting to have to rush forward with Hambecker and subdue Victor. He opened the door and the air whooshed out of me. It was empty.

"Looking for me?"

We turned to find Victor had crept up behind us. He was holding a gun to Claire Perkins.

Victor motioned us down the stairs and followed us, his arm tight around Claire, gun to her side. We emerged from the kitchen into the night. Victor directed us to Claire's Subaru, where I had to maneuver myself over the shifter so Hambecker could get in and drive. Victor and Claire sat in the back, Victor keeping the gun low, but visible to us in the front seat. He was in control.

"Eighty-nine north," was all the direction Victor gave Hambecker and we rode in silence out Route 110 and up Route 14 to 107 and the interstate. Once on the interstate my curiosity got the better of me and I turned to the back.

"What were you doing at Ronnie's, Claire? No offense, but you were the last person I expected to see."

"I'll tell you later." She shot her eyes at Victor. "But believe me if I'd have known what was up, I'd have stayed home."

No duh.

When we were approaching Randolph, Victor said, "Exit four," and we drove up into Randolph Center and past the Vermont Technical College. He had Hambecker stop in front of a small cape overlooking the valley and tapped something into his cell. A couple of minutes later Ronnie came running out of the house and climbed in the back seat next to Claire.

"Drive over to Route 14 and head north." He directed Hambecker for another thirty minutes until we pulled up in front of an isolated horse barn. There were no cars, no sign of horses, just a huge barn with an indoor riding arena attached. Victor had us drive into the deserted arena where we got out of the car.

"No horses," said Ronnie sadly as we walked into the stable portion of the barn. She was right; just a long line of empty stalls on either side of the aisle. The tack room was standing open and we went in, Hambecker, Claire and I sitting on an old bale of hay covered with a Navaho patterned blanket. Victor locked the door we'd come through and then handcuffed Claire to my other wrist so my arms were crossed in front of me. Not the most comfortable position I'd ever been in.

Ronnie was tidying, hanging up old halters and bits of left behind tack that remained in the room. She picked up feed bags and old soda cups and dumped them into a trash barrel, clucking and talking softly to herself. Victor went to talk to her, voice low.

Claire took advantage of the moment and leaned into me. "I walked in on Ronnie cleaning the other night. I startled her and she knocked over her mop bucket. The minute she saw the mess on the floor she pulled diapers out of her bag and laid them on the water. They were disposable ducky diapers."

I looked at Ronnie, her head bent, listening to Victor. "Are you sure?" I asked Claire.

"Without a doubt."

"Did you hear that?" I asked Hambecker. "Ronnie uses ducky diapers to sop up spills."

"I heard. Let's worry about that later." His voice was so low I almost couldn't hear him. "Be ready. Tell

Claire."

We sat for a minute longer, until Victor looked deep in conversation with Ronnie. Then I felt Hambecker tense and he laced his fingers in mine. The next minute we were running through a small doorway, Hambecker dragging me and Claire holding my wrist from behind. I hoped like hell that we weren't running into a dead end, like the bathroom, but it was stairs leading upward.

"Wait! I can't run like this," I hissed. Claire ducked under my arm so that my arms uncrossed. Better, but running while handcuffed was no piece of cake. We went up the stairs like the three stooges.

I was nowhere near as fit as Hambecker, and I couldn't keep up. He pretty much pulled us up the stairs and into a hayloft, with Claire pushing from behind. We ran to the rail overlooking a drop into a huge indoor riding arena. Hambecker would have been able to take the fall, but there was no way I was vaulting the railing. I'd have broken my leg for sure.

"Run." He headed right as I headed left, his greater bulk snapping me back. I slipped and fell, my arms nearly popping out of their sockets. I scrambled to my feet with their help, tears leaking from my eyes. We ran the length of the building, until we reached open wooden steps leading down. Ronnie and Victor close behind us. Hambecker grabbed a bale of hay and rammed it in the top of the stairs behind us on the way down.

"Head start." He pulled us onward out into the arena toward a huge set of doors on the far side. A shot sounded and a bullet hit the dirt inches from me. We reversed direction and ran back under the loft and through a passageway to the main barn. We were three quarters of the way down the barn.

"This way." Hambecker grabbed my wrist and pulled me along.

"I can't breathe," I panted.

"Don't talk."

We burst out the doors into a paddock. The grass was high, four feet at least. It was obvious to me that it had been a while since it had been used. We ran three-across through the pasture toward the road and when we heard a gunshot from the direction of the barn Hambecker said, "Crouch down," and the three of us ran doubled over, trying to stay beneath the level of the weeds.

I was trying to stay calm. I didn't want to get shot. We reached the fence and Hambecker motioned me down. We slithered under the bottom rail, sat and slid into the ditch lining the road and splashed along as quietly as we could. Not that noise mattered, we'd be sitting ducks when Victor and Ronnie caught up.

Hambecker pulled his cell from his pocket and tapped in 911. He started to hand it to me then shook his head. "You don't know where we are either." He spoke into the phone and handed it to me. "Hang on to this. Don't turn it off." I took the phone and kept splashing along behind him, but my arm kept jerking with the pull of the handcuff, so I handed it off to Claire.

At a bend, Hambecker took the opportunity to pull us onto the road and we ran faster. Claire breathed hard beside me and I watched where I was putting my feet. Dirt roads are full of pitfalls like rocks waiting to sprain the ankles of the unwary. My shoulders ached from the constant yanking and my feet were leaden and soggy. But living was high on my list of priorities, so I forced myself to keep going.

We came to a cross roads and Hambecker slowed and looked at the signs. "Do you know where we are?" he asked.

I looked at the signs, digging in my memory. "I think we're in Randolph Center. There are a bunch of horse farms up here."

"She's right," Claire said. "We're north of exit four."

"Which way should we go?"

I thought a minute. "Tom's on his way?"

"Yeah."

"Then stay on this road. He'll find us faster."

A shot rang out.

"Unless we're dead. Come on."

The road started downhill. It was heavily graveled and I slipped on the rocks.

"Slow down!" But it was too late—my foot began to slide, there were a few seconds of *oh shit* while I was in midair, and then I was on the ground with Hambecker on top of me and Claire on top of him.

"Get off already, I can't breathe!"

Claire slid down to my right and Hambecker grunted and rolled off flat on his back in the dirt, my arm once again pulled across my body.

"I'm getting real tired of this," I said.

"More than just your arm is going to hurt," Victor's voice came from above us. He and Ronnie were standing above us, breathing hard. The gun in Victor's hand pointing straight at my heart. I closed my eyes.

"Don't close your eyes," Hambecker hissed at me.

"I don't want to see it coming," I said.

"Keep your eyes open. Trust me on this."

"I'm lying on a dirt road, about to be shot and you want me to trust you?"

"Stop whining and just do it."

I squinted up at the two of them, hating them as much as I'd ever hated anyone. *That's right bitch*, I thought, *you're going to have to look me right in the eyes when you shoot me.*

The surprising thing was that it seemed to bother him. He lowered the gun. "Get up."

We struggled to get up out of the dirt. The longer we were shackled together the worse we got at keeping ourselves untangled. Finally Hambecker said, "Stop," and balanced in a squat. He took my hand and helped me up as he and Claire stood. "You want to take these off of us?" he asked.

"Are you kidding? I need the comic relief. I'll give you the keys before we leave," Victor waved the gun in the direction of the barn. "Get moving."

"You're bleeding." Ronnie pointed to Hambecker's shoulder. It was damp with blood.

"Your brother shot me."

"You'll live," Victor said. "Let's go."

We trudged back toward the stable. I was worried about Hambecker's shoulder and listening for the cops because while I used to kind of like Ronnie and Victor, I didn't anymore.

I was disappointed when we reached the big barn with no sign of the cavalry. Victor put us in a box stall, found a padlock in the tack room and put it on the latch so we couldn't get out.

"I'll put the key to the padlock on the floor over here," he said. "So that when someone finds you, they can get you out."

"Wait. Where are you going?" I asked. "I thought

you needed protection."

"It's taking too fucking long. By the time there's a plan in place, Ledroit will have killed both of us.

"Why did you kill Albin Shvakova?" I asked.

"Hughie doesn't kill people." Ronnie's head popped over the stall wall. She must have been sitting on the floor outside.

"Somebody killed him, Ronnie. I know you don't want it to be your brother, but who else could it be?" I wanted to go to the door and talk to her privately, but privacy was impossible while handcuffed.

"Me." Ronnie was resolute. "That man would have killed Hugh, so I shot him instead."

My eyes sought Victor. His eyes were locked with Hambecker's, some understanding forming between them.

"Aren't you forgetting something?" Hambecker asked. "Keys?"

"Oh." Victor walked back, pulling the handcuff keys from his pocket. "Here," he said, and tossed them into the stall. They went straight over our heads and out the window.

"Fuck." Hambecker looked as if he could kill Victor.

"Sorry," Victor said, and shrugged. Then he turned and jogged away from us down the barn.

We lined up against the far wall and slid down into the sawdust that remained in the stall. I leaned against Hambecker and Claire leaned against me.

"They could have left us something to drink," I said.

"It won't be long now," Claire patted my arm. "We can take you to emergency and get you drugs."

"Drugs. Yeah, that would be good." I closed my

eyes, willing the pain in my head to subside.

An hour later we heard voices outside the barn. We got up off the cold cement and went to the bars, shouting "Hey!" and "We're here!" until they reached us.

Tom took one look and choked back a laugh.

"It's not funny, Tom," I said.

"You're bleeding. Let me call the ambulance."

"Yes." Hambecker and Claire said together.

"No." I said.

"The key to the lock is supposed to be on the floor down the aisle," I said, being my normal, helpful self. "Getting us out of here might be a good start."

A search of the aisle produced no such keys. Victor must have forgotten to leave it after he'd thrown the handcuff key out the window. Tom got the bolt cutters out of his patrol car and snapped the lock. Then he released us from the cuffs.

My wrists were raw, but at least I didn't have a bullet in me. Hambecker lost no time in getting away from us. He shot out the stall door and down the barn like a man on a mission. I don't know why it hurt my feelings, but it did. I thought we'd done pretty well, better than most people who were handcuffed together, but I guess he didn't agree. I didn't get a chance to ask him; he'd gone off with one of the other state troopers by the time I got outside.

Steve Leftsky took me to the emergency room to have my temple cleaned up and my wrists wrapped and then he took me home. I finished a container of Greek yogurt I found in my fridge and then felt so sleepy that I went to bed without writing anything down.

I opened my eyes to Beagle Annie tugging on my sweat pants and the smell of hot smoke making me cough. Some part of my brain sprang into panic, but I was having trouble keeping my eyes open. I rolled off the bed and fell onto the floor when my legs wouldn't hold me up. Roaring came from the stairs and when I forced my eyes open I could see the reflection of the flames. My head pounding I crawled to the door. Flames already consumed the other end of the hall. I slammed the bedroom door closed.

I lay on the floor, willing my body to cooperate while Annie howled in my ear and jabbed me with her nose. I drifted until she got a mouthful of my hair and pulled.

"Annie, stop." I forced myself over to the window and pulled myself up, leaning on the sill. I rested my face on the window but I couldn't think what to do next. Someone was yelling but all I wanted to do was sleep. Beagle Annie nipped me.

"Yow! That hurts. "I opened the window and gingerly touched the metal porch roof. Still cool.

"Annie! Out!" She jumped gracefully out onto the roof. I rolled myself out and lay flat on the roof. There were voices urging me to move. I needed just a minute. One minute to clear my head. Beagle Annie grabbed my pant leg, and I was going to tell her to give me a minute but Max's voice was in my ear.

"Come on, little girl. We've got to get you to safety."

I was lifted, and handed off to someone on a ladder.

"Annie!" Where was my dog?

"I've got her. Don't you worry," Max said.

My chest was so constricted I could barely breathe. Thoughts of Ranger, Diesel and Hank somewhere in the flames on the main floor seared through me. *Wake up!* Vehicles pulled into the door yard as more volunteer firefighters arrived ahead of the fire engines. I could hear the wail of the emergency vehicles approaching.

The firefighter set me on the ground near my truck. I took Beagle Annie from Max but she launched herself from my arms and raced onto the porch running back and forth emitting a high pitched howl. I started to get to my feet, my brain at least had started to cooperate, but Max grabbed me from behind.

"No, Bree, You can't go up there."

I struggled against Max, crying and screaming for him to let me go. Fire engines rolled into the drive, and then an explosion from my kitchen that burst the windows outward. Beagle Annie ran back to me and I held her tightly as she squirmed, yowling and nipping at me. When she bit my hand, I lost my grip and she jumped from my arms and ran through the door behind a firefighter and into the fire.

"No!" My heart stopped beating. I tore myself from Max but another set of strong arms wrapped around me pulling me away, back.

"Easy." It was Tom's voice in my ear. "There's nothing you can do."

"The dogs." The words were so distorted by the sobbing I didn't think he'd be able to understand me.

"We'll look for them, Bree, but don't hold out hope. I'm sorry."

I stood next to the fire truck and watched my house burn. The ambulance came and the paramedics made me sit down, but I refused to leave. The interior of the house was engulfed. It was shingled in asbestos and from what the fire fighters were saying it just made everything worse. There was nowhere for the heat to escape making it impossible for them to get inside.

A spark caught the chicken coop on fire. I stumbled to the enclosure, fighting the gate in my haste and was able to open the hen house door before I was dragged away again. Restrained by a fire fighter and then an EMT, I fought to calm myself but the horror overwhelmed me. I wanted to be helping, to be *doing* something, not helplessly watching my life erased by fire.

A small shadow moved through the door, small and black against the red smoke of the interior. A firefighter scooped her up and brought her to me. It was Beagle Annie with Annabelle Cat in her mouth. They were both a mess, singed and black. I couldn't tell if Annabelle Cat was alive, but Beagle Annie was whining.

"Good Girl, Annie." I gently patted the top of her head, the one place that didn't look burned and sore. Her tail thumped and she looked at me with her black rimmed beagle eyes. Tears gathered behind my eyes and constricted my throat. An EMT came to look at her. She knelt and gently removed Annabelle Cat from

Beagle Annie's mouth. She listened to Beagle Annie's breathing and placed an oxygen mask over her nose, but I knew from the techs movements that she didn't hold any hope.

"Sweet, sweet, dog," I said. "Best dog. Brave, brave girl."

Beagle Annie's tail thumped twice more and then lay still. Her breathing stopped. I closed her eyes and stood up, needing to be out of the hustle and noise, away from all this. I practically ran to the barn forcing my legs to cooperate. I let myself into an empty stall, slumped into a corner. Curled in the hay. I almost didn't recognize the keening was coming from me. I rocked and sobbed. Dust and grief clogging my throat, my face wet. I shattered, and broke and pounded my fist against the sawdust-covered concrete. I knew who had done this, and she would pay.

Eventually Hambecker found me. I was curled on the floor, numb. Not sleeping, but not really awake, I didn't really become aware of him until he touched my shoulder. I blinked at him, unsure why he was there. He pulled me to him holding me close and I cried again while he rocked me in his arms and made soothing noises.

When I stopped crying he picked me up and carried me from the stall.

"I can walk." More of a croak than anything, I wasn't sure he'd understood me.

"Just because you can, doesn't mean you should." He took me to his SUV and set me in the passenger seat. "I'll be right back."

I watched him walk to a group of people standing in the smoke and say something. Tom stepped away from the group and they stood head together for a minute before Hambecker turned and came back. He got in and turned the key. "I'm taking you to Meg's," he said.

I sat curled in the seat, numb and raw and leaned my head against the window. I misjudged the distance and my head bounced against the window. Stabbing pains shot through my temple. *Good. I should hurt.* I willed Hambecker to hit some deeper ruts, bounce harder down the hill as if the pain in my head could erase the pain in my heart.

Hambecker took me to Meg's and carried me upstairs to her spare bedroom. My face was bleeding again and he cleaned it with warm water and soap, applied antibiotic ointment and bandages. Then he pulled off my boots, turned down the covers and put me into bed, fully dressed.

I wanted to tell him that I couldn't sleep, that I was hurting too much, but I couldn't bring myself to talk. There just didn't seem to be any point in it. He pulled the rocking chair over to the bed, sat and held my hand. I rolled toward him, curling around his hand. My link to sanity.

"I'm going to kill her." It came out a dusty croak.

"I know. Now sleep."

I did eventually sleep, and when I woke up Hambecker's hand was still in mine. He sat in the rocking chair, his eyes closed. Morning had come and gone, the clock on the bedside table showed it was past two in the afternoon. I released Hambecker's hand and sat up, feeling the stiffness and pain in my body. I had a burn on the back of my hand that I didn't remember getting.

I was halfway to the door, walking as quietly as I could when Hambecker said "Where are you going?"

"To the bathroom."

"And after that?"

"To kill Michèle Ledroit."

"Hmmm. I thought so. Come back in here first, and we'll make a plan."

I nodded and left. The mirror in the bathroom was not kind. I had bruising and lacerations and bandages on both sides of my head. There was a burn on my cheek and my hair was sticking out all over. The circles under my eyes made me look as though someone had been using me as a punching bag and there were black soot marks everywhere. I was disheveled and disreputable and I didn't care.

There was a knock at the door.

"Yeah?"

"I'm tossing in a towel. Get a shower and Meg will bring you up some clean clothes."

The door opened and a towel appeared. Not that I cared what I looked like, but it would feel nice to be clean. When the water hit my hair the smell of smoke intensified. I gritted my teeth and kept washing refusing to dwell on the images that flashed through my brain.

Instead of making me feel better, the shower made me crankier. I got out prepared to pick up my stinky clothes and find Meg, but my dirty clothes had disappeared and on the counter was a stack of clean things. I almost cried when I saw the underwear, socks and bra were brand new. *Toughen up*, I told myself. *Crybabies don't get to kill wicked old women.* I pulled on Tom's sweats and T-shirt and went back to the spare room to get my boots.

Chapter Thirteen

My boots were gone, the bed had been stripped clean and the quilt from my bedroom was folded neatly on the dresser. It should have been charred to a crisp, but here it was. I picked it up and put my face in it. It had been cleaned so it smelled fresh, which was nice but not what I was expecting. I sat on the bed with my face buried in the last thing I had of my Grammy's and cried for the loss of the cat hair and dog smell that I used to complain about, but now wanted more than anything.

When Hambecker came to find me I was curled on the naked mattress, my arms wrapped around the quilt, my face still hidden in the fabric. The crying had stopped, mostly because I was too exhausted to continue. Hammie sat on the bed and caressed my hair for a while.

"Come on, Trouble, we need to get some food in you. Then we need to make a plan." He tugged the quilt out of my arms and laid it on the end of the bed and taking my hand he led me downstairs to the kitchen. Meg was chopping celery and when she heard us come in she set down the knife and wrapped her arms around me.

"I'm so sorry, Sweetie. Tom's already got the team out there investigating; we'll find who did this."

"I know who did it."

Meg looked startled. But a shrill bark from upstairs

distracted her. "I almost forgot." She walked to the stairs and called up them, "Sara, honey, bring him down."

A door opened and the clicking of nails on the hardwood floor was followed by a little brown body dashing down the stairs. Beans' feet slid out from under him as he rounded the corner full speed and hurled himself at me. I caught him and held him to me, laughing and crying at the same time.

"I'd forgotten he was here," I said, sniffing. "Beans, you lucky, lucky dog."

Beans licked my face and made whining noises that told me he'd missed me, then Meg insisted that I sit down at the table so she could feed me. Beans rolled himself into a ball in my lap while I ate scrambled eggs and toast, because Meg claimed I needed comfort food that wouldn't upset my stomach. I was surprisingly hungry. I ate everything on my plate plus a banana.

"That's enough for now," Meg said, "you'll make yourself sick. And dinner's only a couple of hours away."

"Where did my quilt come from?" I asked, and was dismayed when my voice caught in my throat. I still couldn't talk about things.

"Max pulled it out of your bedroom; the stupid man could have been killed." Meg banged a pot in the sink. "Everyone knows you don't run into a fire."

I made a note to tell him off next time I saw him, and then give him a hug.

Hammie and I took Beans out onto the deck. It was a pretty afternoon, not too hot, and a fresh breeze blew the fragrance of the river mixed with the flowers from Meg's garden. I sat on the bench, watched Beans sniffing around the planters and tried not to fall into despair. Hammie sat beside me, just touching at the shoulder and hip. A solid and comforting presence.

"Shouldn't you be out rounding up criminals?"

"I'm taking a few days off."

"Oh." I leaned against him a little and when he slid his arm around my shoulder I leaned more, resting my head on his shoulder. "The sky is very blue today."

"Yep." He planted a kiss on the top of my head. "I've never been more scared than when I heard your house was on fire last night. I promised myself that if you were okay I would stop pretending to myself that I didn't like you." He tightened his arm. "Don't ever scare me like that again. I don't think I could survive it."

"I didn't mean to." Tears were burning the backs of my eyes. "Why wasn't Ledroit in jail? I thought we were safe. A couple of days you said. She wasn't even in there one night."

"I'm sorry, Bree. We underestimated her influence. And she has a lot of money behind her. The Sheriff's department was out gunned by a big city lawyer and a lot of bluff."

"Can we talk about something else? Because I really don't think I can stand it if I'm going to start crying again."

"What would you like to talk about?"

I looked up him. "How about how long I've been waiting for you to kiss me again? I'm beginning to worry you didn't like it."

He leaned down and pressed his lips to mine. It was a sweet kiss that deepened into something more until I lost my breath and clung to him like a drowning woman.

"Nope," he said when our lips parted, "I liked that

just fine."

He held me close and we sat together, not talking for a long time. I felt the ache in my heart lighten just the tiniest bit and thought about closed doors and open windows. Little wisps of cloud covered the sun for a few moments at a time, bees buzzed around the flowers and the birds sang in the trees. Beans puttered around until Meg's pack came rushing out and then he ran around the house with them. Hambecker disentangled himself from me and got up. He stretched.

"You're just doing that to show off your muscles," I said.

"Gotta make sure to keep you interested." He held out his hand. "Come on. Let's go inside."

We held hands as we walked back into the kitchen where Meg was cutting up potatoes. She looked up. "It's about time. I was ready to give you both a smack."

I grinned sheepishly at her but Hammie said, "You can't rush these things," and pulled me into the living room. We sat on the couch and he turned toward me and took my hands.

"I promise you, we will get Ledroit. It will take some time, but I promise we will get her."

I nodded and leaned into him. "That's good," I said quietly, "because if we don't, then I will."

He looked me in the eyes and nodded. He believed me, and that was a good thing.

For a couple of days, Hambecker refused to leave

my side. I had to negotiate bathroom breaks and showers. He was so sweet and funny that I found it hard to be annoyed. He slept fully dressed curled around me under my Grandma's quilt the first night, but refused my advances. "There are kids in the house," was all he would say. And to tell the truth, that just made me want him all the more.

He went into town with me, standing guard at the office while I worked on my story. When well-wishers tried to bring me things, he took the gifts, thanked them, and very gently turned them away. I pretended not to notice, but I was grateful, because one sympathetic face would be enough to shatter me into a million little pieces. I was holding myself together, but only just.

The heat was making me irritable so Hambecker drove Beans and me to Frosty's Ice Cream. Beans got a vanilla creamy in a dish, I got Deer Tracks in a cone dipped in chocolate and sprinkled with jimmies. Hambecker even broke down and ate a baby-sized creamy twist, despite the fact he *never* ate sweets. We sat on the picnic benches near the river and I smiled while I planned revenge.

We spent time walking along the river, and sitting on rocks while the water swept around us, just listening to the sounds of the water and the rocks and the wind rushing through the trees. The pain of losing my home and my animals didn't go away, but the ache in my chest became familiar, part of who I am.

Hambecker drove me and Beans up Royalton Hill, my heart started hammering as we neared my road, but we didn't turn up it, and my heart settled. And when we got to Silver Lake Hambecker rented us a paddle boat. Beans sat in my lap as we paddled past the state beach, and the town beach where people were eating picnics in the grass. They waved. It was such a normal thing, people waving even though they might not know you at all, and we waved back, but all the time I was hiding the murder in my heart. She would die.

We were paddling back toward the dock as the sun was setting behind the mountains and shadow was starting to fall over the lake when Hambecker asked, "How's the story coming?"

"It's almost done, I just don't know if I should try and compress the whole thing into one article or serialize it across several weeks."

"You really think people are going to want to read about this over weeks and weeks? Fill one paper and let it go."

"What do you know about what people want to read? You haven't read a paper a day in your life." I punched him in the arm, hard.

"Ouch!" Hambecker grabbed his shoulder in mock agony and while he was goofing around he managed to lose his balance and fall overboard. Beans jumped off my lap and stood in his seat barking down at him. Laughter bubbled out of me. I had to wipe the tears from my face.

"Are you going to sit there laughing all day, or can I get some help here?"

I clambered over to his side of the little boat, setting Beans on the seat behind me, and reached out my hand to Hambecker. He grabbed my hand, yanked and the next thing I knew I was in the water with him.

"You turkey!" I splashed him as hard as I could. He splashed back. I lunged at him, climbing on his back, laughing so hard I could hardly breathe. Hambecker submerged and I let go but he twisted and pulled me under, pulling me to him. He kissed me under the water. I wrapped my arms and legs around him, anchoring my fingers in his hair until I was dizzy with the kiss and lack of air. He kicked us up so that we popped up out of the water clinging to each other and gasping for air.

Beans was barking excitedly, hopping up and down on his front feet and Hambecker laughed, tipping his head back, his arms still wrapped tightly around me.

"We'd better go back to the boat before Beans tries to rescue us," I said. "He doesn't know he's too small to pull us ashore."

"Can he even swim?" He looked at Beans.

"Like a fish," I said.

Hambecker kissed me again. "Next time we leave the dog at home."

Hammie pushed me up onto the paddle-boat and then placed his palms on the deck and lifted himself up until he was able to slide his knees on board.

"Show off."

"Gotta keep you interested." He smiled that wicked half smile that turned my insides to mush.

"Oh, I'm interested."

Hambecker reached over and pulled me tight up against him and we paddled for the dock.

I got up the next day resolved to go look at the house. There wasn't anything that really needed doing, Max had been taking care of the horses, and he'd gathered the surviving chickens and added them to his coop, but I wanted to go. I needed to see the damage for myself.

Hambecker was at the barracks with Tom. He may be taking time off from work, but he did need to start checking in regularly on the Hart/Puccini/LeDonne/Ledroit case. The Ledroit Case could have been called the MacGowan Case as far as I was concerned. It was my life that had been altered, but Tom didn't see it that way. He didn't want anyone getting too emotionally involved and going off half-cocked. Especially me. And I agreed with him, to his face.

Meg took me up the hill. We stood in my drive awestruck by the devastation. The smell shocked me. It caught in my throat and made my eyes tear. It was acrid and invasive and disheartening. The shell of the house still stood, sided with asbestos shingle that wouldn't burn. The porch was gone. Every door and every window had been blown out. I moved to where I could see inside, although the smell just about knocked me over. The inside was a hollow hole. Black and empty, at least from where I stood. Everything gone. On the far side of the house the wooden chicken coop had burned to the ground leaving the metal roof warped in the blackened remains. Beyond the hen house was a mound of fresh dirt.

I looked at Meg. "Is that…?" I couldn't finish.

"Yeah. Tom had your animals gathered after the fire inspector gave the okay. They buried… them." All that was left of them was left unsaid, but images came to me anyway.

"What's that?" Scuffling and something almost like bird calls was coming from behind my truck.

"Don't know," Meg said. "You don't think it's an injured chicken, do you?"

"I don't know what that is." We walked around the back of Meg's car to give us some distance from whatever it was.

"Skunk!" Meg jumped and ran back around her car. "Get away! It'll spray and our cars will stink for days."

"It's just Stripes. He's probably wondering why no one is feeding him. I'll drop in on Max and ask him to do it."

"You don't need to drop in, I'm here. Saw you drive up." Max was coming up the drive looking a little more disheveled than usual. His hair was curling up in grey wisps around his head and one side of his button down shirt was un-tucked.

"Max!" I threw my arms around him. "Thank you so much for saving me." I backed off and smacked him on the arm. "I can't believe you went into a burning building for my quilt. You could have been killed!"

"I've been around fire plenty, missy. I knew what I was doing. I knew that quilt was your Grandmother's and I wasn't about to let it burn when it would take thirty seconds to pull it out of there."

I hugged him again. "Thank you so, so much," I whispered in his ear. "You'll never know how much that means to me."

"I have an inkling." He wiped his eyes. "Dang soot still floating around. Anyway, I didn't do nothing anybody wouldn't have done. You were already on the porch roof when I got here. Wicked bad fire. I'm sorry Bree."

"Well, it had some help. The place was doused in accelerant before it was lit. Tom thinks I was drugged."

Stripes came snuffling around our feet. Meg squeaked, "No!" and got in her car. Max bent down and petted the skunk.

"I've been feeding him, but he's wicked distraught. I think he misses Diesel, Bree."

"You handle him, Max?"

"Sure. I get a little skunky, but he never threatens to spray. You should have his scent glands removed; he'd make a fine pet."

"I don't know. If I did that, he couldn't defend himself." I looked at the creature rubbing against Max's legs like a cat.

"He's already dependent on you, Bree. Sure, he lives in the wild, but you already feed him. And since the house burned he's been hanging around moping. Mourning for his friend."

"I'll think about it, but I can't take him to Meg's. The dogs would kill him. Maybe when I have a place of my own again."

"He could come live with my cats."

"Max, it's not something I can arrange right now. I'm sorry, but I can't focus on him."

"How about I just take him on up to my house. He can live in the barn with the outside cats; I don't think the missus will fuss about that. And we can figure out the rest when you're settled."

I hugged him again. "Thank you. You always take care of me."

Max looked at the ground. "Well now, you take care of me too. That's what neighbors are for."

He left soon after, tucking Stripes under his arm like there wasn't any danger of getting sprayed at all. Meg got out of the car and came to stand by me.

"That man is bat shit crazy. Picking up a wild

skunk. It could be rabid."

"Stripes isn't rabid. The vet came out and immunized him when he first adopted me. Max is right. I should have him de-skunked. He'd be a good companion for Beans."

Meg started for the car. "I'm heading home. You coming?"

"I'll be there in a few minutes. I'm going to take a look around. I'll bring my truck down the hill."

I waved as she drove away, and went to stand by the grave of my animals. My companions, really. My family. I squatted and put my hand flat on the dirt. "I'm sorry. I'm so, so sorry I couldn't save you." And I spoke their names. "Beagle Annie, Tank, Ranger, Diesel, Annabelle Cat." Tears ran down my face and watered the dirt. Then I went to the barn and got my wheel barrow, pushing it to a rocky spot at the bottom of the pasture. I gathered as many stones as I thought I could push up the hill. Sweat dripped off me as I muscled the load to the grave. I unloaded the rocks onto the grave and went for more.

I lost count of the number of times I went back for more rocks, but I didn't stop until every inch of fresh dirt was covered and the pile was a good two feet high. Then I rolled the barrow back into the barn, I glanced into the tack room as I went to grab my spare keys and saw the dog beds in a line under the saddle racks. My mind filled with the image of the four of them lying there, keeping watch while I polished bridles, with Annabelle Cat curled on a saddle above them.

Rage filled me, and burned.

Hambecker found me sitting on the rocks with my hands and feet in the water. I had blisters on my palms and the cold water of the White River was taking the sting away. He moved my dusty shoes away from the edge and squatted down next to me. He looked uncomfortable in his heavy work boots, black jeans and a buttoned-up button-down shirt.

"Trouble," he said.

"Hambecker."

"How long have you been down here?"

"Not too long. Take off your shoes and stay awhile," I said.

"Not really my style, but thanks for the invitation."

"You're just going to squat there until I'm ready to go?"

"You have your own vehicle. I don't have to wait until you're ready."

I smiled the sweetest, most accepting smile I could manage under the circumstances. "I'll see you back at Meg's I'll be there for dinner."

Hambecker sighed and unlaced his work boots. He sat on his butt and pulled them off. "I'm going to regret this," he said and plunged his feet in the water.

"You're supposed to roll up your pants." I lifted one leg from the water. "So they don't get wet."

"Again, not my style."

I watched the river slide past his legs, the fabric wicking the water up toward his knees and shrugged. If I was to be truthful the whole pant-leg-in-the-water thing was kind of sexy, and my heart did little flip-flops over the fact he'd put his feet in the water at all. I was turning into an idiot where Hambecker was concerned. I leaned into his shoulder and caught his smile.

"Hammie."

"Hmm?"

"Nothing, I was just saying your name. You forgot to tell me not to call you that."

"I'm finding that futile. I've surrendered. You win."

"No, that's not right. You can't surrender yet. Try again." I paused. "Hammie."

"Don't call me that, Bella."

"Ugh. I hate being called Bella. Rewind. Hammie?"

"Don't call me that, please."

"That's better. I think I'll call you Hammer instead." I laughed at my own humor and was surprised to see him considering the nickname.

"You want to call me Hammer?"

"Maybe *The* Hammer."

His lips twitched until he couldn't hold it in and he grinned. "The Hammer?"

"It was that or Hamster, and I didn't think you'd appreciate that as much."

"Hamster? Yeah, no. Hammer I can live with."

"You don't want me to call you Hammie anymore?"

"No. You can call me Hammie if you want. As long as we're not in public. I don't want it spreading."

I smiled. "So it would be my special name for you? The thing I call you in intimate moments?"

"Don't push it, MacGowan."

"Is this another one of those door and window things?"

"Something like that." He put his arm around me.

"I'd like to kiss you again now, if that's alright?"

"Let's get something straight right now, shall we? You never, never have to ask me if you can kiss me. Is that..." But I didn't get the chance to finish because he'd taken my face in his hands and my mind shut down.

After what seemed like both and eternity and an instant—sorry, but when my mind shuts down I can only come up with clichés—Hambecker broke off the kiss.

"Let's get out of here before someone shows up and tells us to get a room."

"Hmm." I looked at the red spots and blisters on my palms. The numbness from the river had worn off and they were hurting again.

"What did you do?"

"I felt the need to cover the dogs' grave with stone." My voice caught and he slid his arm around me. "I guess I let my hands get soft. Been letting Max do more than his share of the work."

Hambecker took my hand and ran his fingers gently over the palm. "I would have helped you."

"I know. It was something I had to do myself. Atonement or something."

"What do you have to atone for?"

"For not being able to save them. For not hearing anything before it was too late." I took in some air trying to keep the tears at bay.

"You were drugged, Bree. And the accelerant was planted when you weren't there. The basement was loaded with hay and wood pallets. Some gasoline was used, but really it probably would have burned fine without it. It was an old home; once the timber started burning there wasn't much to stop it. The animals would have died of smoke inhalation, not from the fire."

"But why didn't they wake me? They should have been howling and jumping on the bed."

He looked down at the water and sighed. "I didn't want to be the one to have to tell you this. It looks as though they were all locked in the basement before the fire was started. Annie was with you so they couldn't get to her."

"Annabelle Cat? She was already dead when Annie went to get her? Damn it!" I dashed tears away. "I want to be able to talk about this without the fucking waterworks."

He hugged me too him with both arms. "Give yourself a break. It's brand new. If you shut down it will just take you longer to recover. Cry now. We'll talk again later."

"I don't want to cry," I sobbed into his shirt. "I hate to cry. It's so girly." But the tears had gotten hold of me and I couldn't stop.

"You are a girl, Trouble, so I wouldn't worry about it." He rocked me while I cried, stroking my hair. I sniffed and choked for a long time trying to calm myself. A horrible empty pain filled me when I cried. As much as I knew I needed to feel it, I didn't want to. It felt like the world would never be the same again.

After a while Hambecker said, "I don't know about you, but my feet are numb. Can we get out of here before they break off and float down river?"

I disengaged myself from Hammie and wiped my face on my dirty t-shirt. We picked up our shoes and walked gingerly over the warm rocks to the dirt patch where the vehicles were parked.

"I hate to make you drive yourself. Do you want to

leave your truck here? We can come back and get it later."

"No. I'm a big girl. I can drive my truck back to Meg's."

He planted a kiss on my head. "I'll see you there."

The ten minutes it took to get to Meg's house was enough for me to pull myself together. What remained in my mind was revenge. I wanted to burn every last thing belonging to Michèle Ledroit. I wondered how difficult it would be to find out how many properties she owned. I'd burn them one by one, shrinking her world as I came for her. Taking out everything she'd ever loved. Fire burned in me and I was going to let it out.

I wasn't sure if I should talk to Hambecker about burning Ledroit or not. I knew he was with me, but there would be constraints. He'd be satisfied with jail. I would not. Although maybe jail, after I'd destroyed her world. But that could escalate into a two-woman war. It would be better to make it final. After I'd destroyed her. That was crucial. She had to be totally devastated before she died. She had to know what she'd done and that I wouldn't let it go. You don't fucking mess with my loved ones.

Chapter Fourteen

I embraced all the clichés that I'd ever heard about anger. It burned hot in me, pushing aside the grief. It vaporized all the civilized, cultured or sympathetic parts that had remained after the fire. The hatred ignited vengeance and gave me the justification to be inhuman. I knew it, I saw it, but I didn't even try to hold on to my humanity. If I let myself think about it for too long it scared me. I didn't think. I grabbed on to the inferno and held it to me.

As for the voice in my head that was saying, "Don't be stupid, it is not in your nature to destroy people…" I ignored it.

At Meg's, I got drawn into the table-setting, food-serving, general-mealtime-chaos that is dinner at the Maverick's. I was sitting across from Hammie. He smiled every time our eyes met until Jeremy said, "Would you two cut it out? I'm trying to eat, for cripes sake."

"Finally! I told you so," Meg said to the room in general without bothering to look up from her plate. Hambecker had the good grace to look sheepish and I could feel the burn on my cheeks. He reached across the table and squeezed my hand, and I think he would have held onto it for the entire dinner, except it was really hard to eat that way. I couldn't cut my food. Tom smiled, but didn't say anything and Sara giggled.

Being with Hammie was nice, but I wasn't feeling it

the way I normally would have. The effervescence that normally filled me when I had a new boyfriend was missing. I chalked it up to the loss of my home and set it aside. I'd just get it later, that's all.

The men cleared the table and the kids loaded the dishwasher, while Meg hand-washed the pots, pans and assorted handcrafted items. I dried and put away. It was the civilized way of doing things and we were all done quickly. The kids went outside and the guys drifted out onto the deck carrying a six-pack of Red Haired Mary from the Freight House.

"Are you all right?" Meg asked me when the kitchen had cleared out.

"You mean besides losing everything I owned and a lot of what was dear to me? Yeah, I'm fine."

"You're not acting fine. But if you say you're okay, I'll go with it. Do you want to shop for new clothes tomorrow? I know the insurance money hasn't come in, but I can give you an advance if you need it."

I looked down at my clothes. I was still wearing Tom's sweats and t-shirt that'd I'd put on yesterday. "God. I probably smell bad, too."

"Not so bad this morning, but whatever you did at the farm… let's just say you're a little ripe."

I blushed. "I'll go take a shower."

"I put a pair of jeans I found at the thrift shop on your bed, a few shirts too. That should do until we go shopping tomorrow. I'd take you tonight but I have the feeling you'd fall asleep in the car."

Showered and changed I joined the others on the back deck with a Village Idiot, my favorite of the FH beers. I sat down on the bench next to Hambecker and leaned into him.

"When can we talk privately?" I asked him quietly.

"A little later?"

I nodded, listening to the river. Meg said something I didn't catch and Tom laughed. It occurred to me that having me here was putting them in danger. I sat up straight.

"What's up?" Hambecker asked, and Tom and Meg both looked at me with barely concealed concern.

"I'm fine. Stop worrying, you guys, you how I hate that. I just realized I'm putting you at risk staying at your house. I should rent a room somewhere."

"Relax," Tom said. "We've thought of that. I don't seriously think that whoever set fire to your house is going to risk burning down our house, but just in case they are that stupid we've taken precautions. It will be okay."

"But the kids..." The thought of fire in the house with the Maverick offspring caused my throat to close and I looked at Meg with tears behind my eyes willing her to understand.

"If it will make you feel better, the kids had planned to visit their Gramma and Gramps anyway. I'll take them there tomorrow. The dogs can stay in the barn," she added as I started to speak. "It will work out. The house is watched. I will not allow my best friend to rent a room somewhere when she just lost her home. I won't. Get it?"

I nodded and swiped at my eyes. The saner part of

me said *let go of the revenge*, knowing that I could lose these people, this home as well, that it could all be burned away. If not by actual fire then by the space revenge would leave where my heart should be.

"Bree," Tom said, "Have you considered doing some grief counseling? You know, seeing someone to help you let go of any anger and guilt you might have?"

"I'm fine, Tom. It just takes time." *And obliterating that bitch.*

"I don't know Bree. You don't seem like yourself." Tom looked unhappy.

"It hasn't even been a week. But if it will make you happy, I'll make an appointment."

Relief flooded his face and a ball of lead settled in my belly. I was lying to my friends. *Okay then, I will make an appointment, once I've done what I need to do.*

We sat on the deck until the sun went down and the mosquitos started to swarm. When we moved inside Hambecker said "I'm going to take Bree upstairs before she falls asleep on the couch."

"Goodnight all, I'm being sent to bed." Secretly I was glad. My body ached from hauling rocks and sorrow.

I crawled into bed and Hammie sat next to me. Worry clouded his face, but he stroked my hair and kissed me on the forehead, not saying what was on his mind. Considering it was probably my state of mind that was bothering him I was glad he kept it to himself.

"I'll see you in the morning."

"Can't you stay? We could both fit in this bed."

"Not tonight. And not with a house full of kids."

"Will you sit here a while longer?"

"Only if you go to sleep. I'm not going to stay if you're going to try and seduce me."

"Oh, poo." I closed my eyes and enjoyed the touch of his hand on my hair. He really was an excellent boyfriend.

The next day brought the removal of the kids to their grandparent's house in Chelsea, and when she got back Meg loaded me into the car and we headed for West Lebanon.

"Have you heard from Lucy lately?" I asked. "Is she still spreading rumors?"

"If she is, it isn't having the intended effect. I guess word got out that someone was trying to ruin us, and the advertisements are flowing in. The free online ads aren't hurting either. We're going to be all right."

"Let's hope Lucy doesn't get it into her head to try something else," I said. "She's always hell-bent on revenge." This made us more alike than I cared to admit.

We abandoned the subject in favor of an argument of the relative merits of Kohl's and JC Penny's. We don't have a lot of shopping choices in our neck of the woods. We very intelligently settled on both. We shopped, ate dinner and shopped some more. We bought clothes and toiletries, picking up a new laptop before heading home. Our men, plus Steve, were eating barbeque chicken on the deck. We joined the fray, laughing and drinking beer and I felt more normal than I had in days.

Beans sat on my lap and licked barbeque sauce

from my fingers, making me laugh. I kissed his smooth little head and he licked my chin. I fought back tears, keeping my head down until I was under control. Beans was able to get under the ice, he warmed me up until I ached for the other dogs. And it confused me. On one hand he pushed revenge out of my heart. On the other he made me think of the pack, which fueled my need to kill Ledroit in cold blood.

I was relieved when the party broke up and I could let down my guard.

Hammie and I sat on the deck after the party had dispersed. It was quiet. If you've never lived in a place without street lights you have no idea what dark is. It's almost a physical presence, cloaking your sight, but heightening your hearing. The river and the frogs were almost deafening.

"We've got a plan," Hambecker said sliding his arm around me. "We should be able to apprehend Ledroit."

"Apprehend? As in catch her and send her to jail?" I could feel panic and disbelief settling over me. I slid away. "For what? Arson?"

"If the plan goes well, we should also be able to get her for the murder in the salon as well." He reached for my hand.

"She didn't kill the guy in the Salon, Ronnie did." The anger was burning again. I welcomed it.

"I mis-spoke. We can get her for smuggling a hitman across the border illegally. That's a major charge."

"I think we should get a list of her properties and burn them first. Then you can do the plan."

"Not going to happen, sweetheart. I know you want revenge but I think you are going to have to settle for incarceration."

I stood up abruptly. "No. It's not good enough. She needs to pay." I moved away from him into the night and walked right into the house.

"Are you okay?"

I ignored the concern in his voice and walked away. Trailing my hand along the side of the house until I reached the door. It was my way or the highway, and if Hambecker didn't agree then that was too bad.

I started the next day Googling properties owned by LeDonne, although she would forever be Ledroit in my head, pretending to myself that burning her business would satisfy the burn of revenge. I looked at satellite photos of a house in Hoboken. I would start there. Doubt pulled at my conscious. What if there were children? Pets? If I burned a house full of animals, was I any better than she was? No. I told myself I didn't care. She would pay. She would suffer like I had suffered.

I found a drycleaner in Brooklyn that was listed under LeDonne and looked to see where it was located. I would have to burn that at night. I would not risk customers. It looked as though there were apartments over top. I would have to figure a way to warn the occupants. Maybe I could call in a gas leak. That could also explain the fire.

"Hey." Claire was in the door watching me. "You look gruesome, what's up?"

I closed the laptop. "Nothing."

"Sorry about the farm." She sat on the bed, sliding

off her shoes and sitting cross-legged. "How are you doing?"

"I'll be fine. It's a lot to take in right now."

"Have you thought about re-building yet?"

"I think I have to wait until the Fire Marshal and the insurance company sign off."

"I don't think the Fire Marshal is going to object to you *thinking* about rebuilding."

"I guess not."

"You could be thinking about what you want to do differently."

"My great-great-grandfather built that house."

"That doesn't mean he did it the way you would. You put in a bunch of windows when you moved in didn't you?"

"And knocked out some walls. Maybe I should put it back the way it was."

"I think you should make it how you like it. Those people are never going to live there again."

"Maybe."

"Or, if you want to reduce your carbon foot print, you could get one of those tiny houses. You know, Tumbleweeds."

"I've never seen them."

Claire nodded at the computer. "Google them. They're crazy small, but cool."

"I'm busy with something else, but I'll put them on my list." *Right after locking an evil woman in her car and burning it.*

"I've got to go cut hair. They finally let me back into the Salon. Drop in on me."

I followed Claire downstairs to the kitchen and saw her shake her head at Meg. It was barely there, but I caught it and it confirmed my suspicions. I grabbed a soda from the fridge and went back upstairs. I'd look into rebuilding later, to throw them off my trail if nothing else.

Later in the day I "borrowed" a Smith and Wesson handgun from Tom's locked gun cabinet—I knew where to find the key—and purchased ammunition for it. I snuck out to target practice behind the barn when the guys were at the barracks and Meg was at the paper. I wasn't a great shot, but not bad either, and at close quarters I couldn't miss. And if I got the opportunity to use the Smith and Wesson, it would be *very* close quarters.

I hid the gun behind the seat in my truck, away from prying eyes and little hands. I made sure it was well camouflaged, wrapped in an old sweatshirt and a paper bag, and shoved under the seat. It would not do for Hambecker or Tom to find it on me.

By evening I had a list of properties to hit, starting with the least personal and ending with burning Ledroit in her car. The lovely house in Hoboken was second to last. She could watch her world being destroyed, each act coming closer to her heart. My own heart was a ball of black ice.

I went downstairs to find the others gathered around the kitchen table heads close together. They looked up when I walked in and Meg at least had the decency to look guilty.

Hammie gestured to a seat. "Come sit with us.

215

We're working on the plan to take down Ledroit."

"No thanks. I'm sure you can manage that without me." I walked past the table, putting myself on the outer exit side of the room. "I'm going to be gone a couple of days," I said. "I need to go to Rhode Island to pick up some new meds for Lucky. Max says he's going downhill."

"Are you taking Beans?" Meg asked.

"No, he'll be happier here."

Tom looked at me strangely. "Since when would Beans be happier here than in the truck with you? He loves to ride."

"But I can't take him all the places I'm going. I don't want to leave him in a hot car."

"Okay," Tom said. "We'll take care of him."

"Thanks. I'll be back the day after tomorrow."

I made my escape from the disapproving faces. Not one of them had believed a word I said. Which made them pretty damn smart. I was getting ready to pull out when Hambecker appeared at my window. I rolled it down, hardening my face.

"Do you want company?"

"No, I'm good."

"You don't want me with you?"

"I thought you and Tom were planning the take-down. Isn't that more important?"

"No. Tom can handle it. If you need me to go with you, I'll go."

"No. It's fine. I need some time to think about what I'm going to do about the house."

"I make a good sounding board." He wasn't pleading, there was something else there. Throwing me a rope, I decided.

"I'll be back soon. Will you be here?" Not that he'd

want me after he found out what I'd done.

"I'll be here, executing the downfall of Michèle Ledroit."

"Good." I reached out the window and grabbed his shirt-front, pulling him close. I leaned out and kissed him like it was the last time ever.

Because it was.

I was maybe half way to New York City when I let myself think about what I was really planning. Sure, I could burn down half of the city in an effort to make her pay, but in the end, it was a life for a life. Or rather, her one worthless life for the five excellent lives she had taken. I stopped worrying about innocent bystanders and toxic smoke and focused on how I would lure Ledroit to me.

It seemed pretty easy, go to Little Italy, ask around for Margaret LeDonne, tell everyone where I was staying and wait for her to come kill me. The tricky part would be killing her first.

I was a little frightened of who I had become. How seemingly easy it was to go from fairly decent to absolutely amoral. The horrible way my animals had died haunted me, I saw nothing redeeming in Ledroit to make me feel guilty about planning to kill her, but I was missing some failsafe, something that would bring me back from the edge, back to the place where killing people was unacceptable.

I checked into a two-star hotel that was clean, but

basic. The people behind the desk didn't seem to pay too much attention to who was coming and going, and I thought that was probably good. I had Tom's Smith and Wesson with me, a stun-gun and pepper spray.

I slept hard and long that night. I let myself sleep in and spent the morning relaxing. I didn't know how long it would take to lure Ledroit, and I wouldn't be able to do much sleeping until I reeled her in.

After a lunch of clam chowder and grilled-chicken panini, I started my stroll. I asked about Margaret LeDonne everywhere, paying special attention to buildings I knew she owned. I told complete strangers I had a bone to pick and where she could find me. I ate spaghetti in the restaurant where she had talked to Victor Hugo Puccini. I was as visible as I knew how to be, talking to strangers and chatting up the waiter.

The walk back to the hotel was leisurely. I looked in windows; I strolled through shops and fingered silk scarves. I tried on a beautiful red dress that made me look exotic. And when I walked through the lobby I said hello to everyone I saw, making the most of what might be my last free moments on Earth. I had no illusions that I would get away with murder. Nor did I think I should.

I went to bed with the handgun, pepper spray and stun-gun under my pillow. It wasn't at all comfortable, which was fine with me, because I needed to be alert.

My grandma woke me. Not literally, she was dead after all, but in my dream she was warning me of danger. I heard the door click shut and was fully awake.

"Grandma?" I said aloud.

"Grandma?" Ledroit snorted. "You think I'm your dead Grandma? How sweet." It was Ledroit's voice, but I couldn't make our where she was in the room.

"Ledroit. Good. I've been looking for you." I had my arsenal at my fingertips.

"Very brave of you. And foolish. You were lucky to live through the fire. And yet here you are, lamb come to slaughter. "

I switched on the bedside light. Ledroit sat in a chair across from the bed, the black barrel of her gun pointed at me. I sat up and slipped my feet into my shoes.

"Don't get ahead of yourself. If you stand up I'll shoot you."

"Fair enough. Do you have any objection to me tying my shoes?"

"You want to die with your shoes on? Be my guest."

I bent and tied.

"You should have told me you found Victor. I would have paid you handsomely." She was amused, like I was some silly child.

"So you could kill him? I don't think so." I pulled the gun into my lap, resting it with the barrel pointing at her chest.

Ledroit smiled. "You are not such a child then. But you will not kill me."

"I will." I willed myself to pull the trigger; it was her or me. Why was neither of us shooting?

"Tell me something," she said. "Why would you put yourself at risk for a complete stranger?"

"He isn't a complete stranger. His sister is a member of our community. Why would I sell out a member of our community?"

"I thought perhaps you were defying me on purpose. This is just sentimentality, you understand nothing."

"I understand that you killed my family—my dogs—and burned down our family home. For no reason other than you could."

"Your dogs were your family? No wonder you are so pathetic. You need family to make you strong. Not a bunch of pack animals fawning all around you. You are like a little girl."

"And you are a spoiled brat having a temper tantrum." Fury had started to burn through me again. My dogs were not pathetic. Their lives meant something. "If something bothers you, you kill someone. And you call *me* a child."

"Enough…" she started.

But I didn't hear anything else. My ears were ringing with fury; I launched myself off the bed, gun in hand. Her gun discharged like a sneeze, it had a silencer on it, but I didn't feel a bullet hit me. I tackled her, sending her backwards and her gun went flying. She fisted me in the leg with something sharp and pain was quick and hot. I smacked her wrist with the gun and she dropped the blade. We rolled off the overturned chair and she grabbed at the gun in my hand, trying to wrest it from me. A telephone cord was plugged into a jack behind her head. I grabbed it and yanked. The heavy seventies phone came flying off the desk and smashed into us. The phone landed on her face, the receiver clubbed me in the ear. I pushed myself up, dropped my knees onto her chest, pulled back the slide to slide a bullet into the chamber and pressed the barrel of the Smith and Wesson into the middle of her forehead.

Ledroits eyes were locked on mine, daring me to kill her. She didn't speak but the sneer on her face told me that she didn't believe I'd do it. I didn't see anything in her eyes to stop me. Not an ounce of remorse or fear. Not a shred of humanity. I took a breath.

The door to the room clicked open. I didn't blink. My eyes were on Ledroit, but I could see the outline of the guy in the doorway with my peripheral vision.

"Hambecker?" I didn't move a muscle. I tightened my finger and slid it down the trigger.

He walked over and put his hand down. "Give me the gun, Bree."

I shook my head. "Can't."

"Give me the gun. If you walk away now, everything will be fine."

"What do you mean, it will be fine? It will never be fine; she burned my grandma's house. She killed my dogs. I will never, ever be fine again." I looked into Ledroit's flat eyes, two-handed the pistol, and straightened by elbows the way my dad taught me.

"Easy." His voice was calm and low. "I know it's hard to see now but you will get back to normal."

"How? How can I go from wanting revenge to being normal? I want to kill her Hammie, I want her to suffer." I relaxed my elbows and thought I saw a flicker of relief in her eyes.

"I know. I want her to suffer too, just not in quite the same way as you do. But you can't do it, Bree. If you do this, you are going to lose more than you already have." His hand landed gently on my shoulder.

"What more is there to lose, Hambecker? What else is there?" I felt a flood of emotion threaten to overwhelm me and pushed it back.

"You could lose me." His voice was in my ear now. His hand sliding down my arm.

"If I kill her you'll leave me?" I stiffened my arms.

"No. I won't leave you." His hand had stopped below my elbow; I saw surprise in Ledroit's eyes.

"Then what? How can I lose you if you won't leave me?" I slipped my finger off the trigger.

"Because you can't be both *Bree MacGowan: murderous bitch intent on ruining her life for the sake of revenge*, and *Trouble MacGowan: the girl who fell madly in love with Richard Hambecker.*" They were both absolutely still.

"I'm not in love." I was confused.

"I know, but you would be." His voice was barely audible.

"I don't understand." He had my attention now.

"You would be in love with me if you could let go of the hatred." His breath touched my cheek.

"I can't. She killed my sweet Ranger. How can I let that go? I won't betray them." My finger tightened. My chest constricted making it hard to breathe.

Chapter Fifteen

"Listen to me." Hambecker said, his voice low and tight. "You wouldn't be betraying them. Those animals lived for your happiness. They wouldn't want you to die a lonely, bitter old woman so that they could be avenged. Choose me. That would honor them. Be happy. Choose me, Bree."

I looked away from Ledroit. There were tears in Hambecker's eyes, so close to mine and I could see the truth in them. There under the sheen of water and years of holding back was the truth. It was the same love I'd seen in Beagle Annie's eyes before she died. The same love I got from my brothers and parents. And I was going to lose it. Not just Hambecker's, I would lose it all.

I pulled the gun back, away from Ledroit's head and took my knees off her chest. There was a flurry of movement, and the room was full of men dressed in full SWAT gear. They had Ledroit up and out of the room so fast it was like she was never there. Even the gun she brought with her was bagged and gone.

I looked up at Hambecker. Calm and cool Richard Hambecker. He looked like he'd been hit by a truck. There was no color in his face and his hands shook as he emptied the rounds from the gun.

The horrible calm in me broke. The pain and regret. The loss and fear flooded back into me, and out in an uncontrollable wail. I threw myself at Hambecker, pounding on his chest and sobbing. He caught and held me. Wrapping his arms around me tight, holding me together when the pain would have torn me apart. I stopped hitting and clung to him with every ounce of strength I had. I cried until I passed out from exhaustion, there, in his arms.

I opened my eyes to Tom and Steve standing in the doorway. Tom was holding a first aid kit. He tossed it kit to Hambecker. "You can do the honors, I'm not asking her to take her pants off."

A cop dressed in black stuck his head in the door behind Tom. "We're taking out the trash. You okay in here?"

"Fine," Hambecker said. "Lock the door on the way out would you, Tom?"

The door clicked shut and Hammie turned to me. "Strip," He said.

"I will not. I will remove my jeans so you can put a Band-Aid on my booboo, but I'm not stripping." I turned my back to undo my pants.

"Just get on with it." I could almost hear him rolling his eyes.

I shucked my pants and he let out a low whistle. "That's nasty. We're going to the ER." He secured a dressing over the wound and I put my pants back on.

"You're looking a little green. Blood make you nauseous?" he asked.

"No. It just decided to hurt again." *Like a son of a bitch.* I breathed through my nose and focused on neither throwing up or passing out.

"Shit." Hambecker picked me up and carried me out of the room.

"I can walk," I said as he took the stairwell down to the first floor.

"No. You can't. I'm not having you pass out and bash your head on the sidewalk."

"It's Hammer time." I grinned. "I was saved by the Hammer."

"Very funny. Hold on for a sec." We'd come out into the underground parking and I locked my arms around his neck while he fished keys from his pocket and beeped the SUV open.

"I'm getting banged by the Hammer." I giggled uncontrollably into his shoulder.

"Not tonight, you aren't." He set me gently in the passenger seat and closed the door.

"Sledgehammer," I sang.

"You been listening to your mother's albums?" He slid into the driver's seat.

"The oldies station. Helps me sleep in strange places. Do you want to be my sledgehammer, Hammie?" I was focusing all my energy on driving him crazy, because if I didn't the pain was going to make me cry.

He sighed. "Do I have to answer that?"

"No 'cause I know you want to be my sledgehammer, don't you?" *Oh my God, my leg feels like it's on fire.*

"Crap, if this is what you're like now, what's going to happen when they give you pain pills?" The tone of his voice indicated he was doing mental eye-rolls.

"Don't worry. I'll just pass out."

True to my word, that's exactly what I did. I gritted my teeth while the doc numbed the four-inch laceration in my leg, which didn't, by the way, make the throbbing go away. When they finally allowed me the narcotics I was happy to let the drugs have their way with me. But not before signing the release papers.

I was back in Hambecker's arms when I woke. We were lying on the bed, his arms wrapped tight around me. I sighed and snuggled into him. Safe. Sane. I felt the ache inside me. It would be with me for a long time. That was fine, I'd be okay. People are built to live with loss.

Hammie stirred. "You were wrong."

"What was I wrong about this time?" I pushed my face into his chest.

"You do love me." His arms tightened around me.

"I know. And someday you'll learn to love me too." I snuggled closer.

"Trouble?" Hambecker's voice was low.

"Hmm?" I was barely awake now.

"I won't."

My eyes opened wide. "Why not?"

"Because I already do." He smiled wide.

I smiled back. "You do what?" I was fishing.

"Love you. I love you." He brushed his lips lightly over mine.

"I know. I just wanted to hear you say it." A bubble of joy expanded in my chest filling me with warmth.

He pulled me close and I dozed there, safe.

Later, when we'd showered, we joined Tom and Steve in the coffee shop across the street. We sat squashed in a large booth. There should have been loads of room for four people, but when three of the four have shoulders like bulldogs… well, let's just say I was having an interesting time getting my fork to my mouth.

"How did you guys find me?" I asked when my order of french fries hit the table. "I was being so sneaky."

"I hate to tell you this," said Tom, "but you're pretty damn transparent."

"Remember the GPS you attached to my car?" Hambecker asked. "I've had one in your truck since I came to town."

"What? Isn't that illegal or something?" I asked, outraged. Well almost outraged, I'd done it to him too, after all.

"Hey, Bree," Steve said through a mouthful of Ruben. "Maybe you shouldn't be so worried about what's illegal, considering what you were up to."

"That's it? You just stuck a GPS on me and followed me around?" It seemed too easy.

"Your browser history helped. It was clear you were after Ledroit." Hambecker forked some mac and cheese in his mouth. "This is good."

"I thought I erased my browser history. Yum, this is good." I took another drink of chocolate shake. "I'm coming here next time I'm in New York."

"Browser history isn't that easy to get rid of," Hambecker said. "You'd have to be a lot more of an expert than you are."

"How come all three of you came? Aren't you and Steve supposed to be *Vermont* State Troopers?" I asked Tom.

"We're off duty," Steve said. "And we didn't know exactly what you had planned. It was going to take more than one person to ditch a dead body."

The ramifications of two cops and a federal agent hiding a body for me left me speechless for a moment.

"But what about the SWAT team. How'd they get involved?" I asked.

"I tracked down Victor. He agreed to turn state's evidence if we protected Ronnie. It was an easy deal to make. With his evidence we're able to arrest her on charges of murder, attempted murder, arson and racketeering. She won't be getting out on bail. This time."

"Getting home is what I'm concerned about now," Tom said. "I think you should let Steve drive your truck."

"You can ride home with me." Hambecker was spooning up the last remains of his pasta.

"I can drive. I just won't take any pain pills." Someone in my head was saying *stupid, stupid, stupid*.

"It's five hours, Bree. That's a long time to be in pain. Why don't you let Steve drive your truck back and you can ride with me. You could sleep the whole way if you want to." Hambecker looked me full in the eyes, face calm but unsmiling.

I thought about this while I chewed on my fries. I'm stubborn, I know this about myself. Independent, too. My immediate response was to say, "No." I'd drive myself. Hambecker was watching me, gauging my response, I thought. I had serious misgivings about dating a federal agent, but I would be heartbroken if I let him go. Crap. I was going to have to compromise. I swallowed.

"I'll ride back with you," I said.

He smiled. And it wasn't a self-satisfied I-know-best smile. It was a soft, she-likes-me-enough-to-give-up-a-little-control smile. It made me feel warm inside.

After we'd finished Tom looked at me. "Ready to do this the legal way?"

"Yeah. I'm ready."

I gave my statement in a scary looking building in the Federal Plaza in Manhattan. I felt shabby in my jeans and t-shirt – I hadn't actually packed for anything other than the take down of Madam Michèle Ledroit. I was escorted to a small room and left to wait by myself while the Law Enforcement Officers—Tom, Steve and Hambecker—went to discuss the case with somebody important.

"Fuck," I said, and then, "Sorry," in case anyone was listening. There wasn't a mirror in the room, but I figured now they had cameras, they probably didn't need to use two-way glass. It definitely felt like an interrogation room. I hadn't taken any painkillers because I wanted to seem alert and trustworthy, and— let's face it—awake, and I regretted that now. My leg throbbed, my head pounded and I was bored.

After sitting primly in the chair for about an hour I gave up, put my head on the table and groaned. "I'm in pain here, people. Maybe whoever's listening could tell someone to put a fire under their ass." I wasn't going to be able to go to sleep as much as I now wanted to. I was uncomfortable and self-conscious.

I was saying, "Hey, y'all, I need to use the ladies' room," when Tom walked in with a very starched and official official.

"MacGowan, what are you doing?" He looked at me like I had two heads.

"Talking to whoever is listening." I said.

Tom looked at the suit. "Is this room bugged?"

"There's a microphone for recording statements, but it isn't on. There's a restroom down the hall on your right." He pointed down the hall.

I got up and fled to the ladies' feeling foolish. When I came out again, all the doors looked the same and I stood in the hall wondering if I should just start knocking on doors or yell for Tom or what. Luckily, before I started either option Tom stuck his head out and motioned me back in the room.

"You thought you were locked in here?" He asked.

"No one said anything to me. They just put me in here and said someone would be in to take my statement. They didn't say I could go down the hall or anything. Can we get this over with Tom? My leg hurts like a son of a bitch."

"Did your medication wear off?" Tom asked.

"I didn't take any. I pass right out—ask Hambecker—every time I take those things. I thought it might be important to be coherent." My eyes stung like I might cry again, but I blinked hard and kept myself together.

The suit who had been studying me as if I was some kind of alien while I talked with Tom finally stuck out his hand. "Senior Agent Andrew Smith," he said. "I'm sorry you were under the impression that you weren't free to come and go. This is a sensitive case and we wanted to get input from Agent Hambecker before hearing what you had to say. If I'd realized you'd been wounded," at this he shot a look at Tom, "I would have seen you first. I understand you were present when the body of Albin Shvakova was found?"

"Yes," I took a breath. What followed was another hour and a half of monolog on my part, punctuated by questions on Agent Smith's part. He was most interested in my version of the take-down.

He eventually released me and escorted me to the cafeteria where he bought me lunch and a soda. "Take your medications," he said. "Agent Hambecker will be down to get you before you fall asleep. Again, my apologies for neglecting you."

"It's okay, I'm fine." I lied. It didn't seem like the right time to complain; he had, after all, just bought me lunch.

"I expect to be seeing you at the trial." He set my tray on a small table in a private corner of the room.

"The trial?" My voice jumped into the soprano register. "I have to go to the trial?" *Of course you have to go to the trial, Bree. You're a witness.* "Sorry, yes, of course. I just hadn't thought about it."

I shook his hand and when he turned to walk away I sat and fished the bottle of oxycodone out of my bag. My head was pounding so hard I didn't think I was going to be able to eat my food, but I took a bite so the narcotic wouldn't go straight to my head. Just what I needed was for Hambecker to find me face down in my lunch tray. I ate what I could and wrapped up the rest for the trip home.

Hambecker arrived before I totally passed out, although I could tell the drugs were taking effect. The pain was subsiding and I was feeling fuzzy and tired.

"Oh hell," he said when he saw me. "Let's get you out of here."

"That is no way to greet your potential girlfriend." I was finding it hard to enunciate my words.

"Maybe not, but let's face it: 'oh hell' is the thing that springs to mind most of the time I see you." He picked up my tray and dumped the trash.

"Gee, I've got such a swell guy! He says the sweetest things to me." I stood up and swayed beside the table.

"Can you be a little quieter? This is where my boss works." He put his arm around me and started to hustle me out.

"I'm sorry, am I too loud?" I leaned over to a smartly dressed woman sitting alone at a table for two. "Am I too loud? I hope I'm not disturbing you."

"Sorry," Hambecker said. "Oxycodone."

The woman smiled at him in a totally inappropriate manner and I was going to have to tell her off but Hambecker whisked me out the door and into an elevator.

"Boy, you really can't handle your sedatives, can you?" He punched the button for the Lobby.

"What do you mean? Just because you don't like what I'm saying doesn't mean I can't handle drugs. If you treated me better, this wouldn't be an issue." I leaned against him. "It's a good thing you're big and strong."

"Why's that?" He frowned down at me.

"Because I think I'm going to sleep now."

The last thing I heard before my eyes closed was, "Oh hell."

It was dark, and the lights from the dash were reflecting off Hammie's face. I looked at the freeway signs, trying to get a bead on where we were, but nothing looked familiar. In fact, it was mostly just dark.

"Where are we?" I asked.

"Sleeping beauty awakes. We're in upstate New York. Passed Albany about thirty minutes ago." Oncoming headlights lit his face. He looked tired.

"I like this way best. Did you have trouble getting me in the car?" I asked.

"Not once I got out of the building. At one point I thought I was going to have to get Agent Smith to come clear me. They wouldn't let me out of the building without pulling my ID. I guess carrying women from the building just isn't done." He smiled.

"How'd you get it out of your pocket?" I imagined him handing me to some poor unsuspecting security guard.

"A security agent had to remove it from my pocket for me. Embarrassed the hell out of her." The glow of the instrument panel lit his face but I couldn't see his expression. He might have been grinning.

"Just think, without me your life would be so boring." I put my hand on his arm. He was so solid.

"Boring. Right. And here I was thinking *normal*." He was smiling again.

"I hate to tell you this, Hambecker, but you're a federal agent. Your life is anything but normal." In fact, it was even less normal than mine. Which was saying something.

"It seems normal compared to this." He took my hand and held it, so I didn't feel the sting of the words.

"If I'm such a pain, why are you still hanging around?" I considered taking my hand back, but didn't.

"Can't help myself? God knows, I tried to stay away." He squeezed my hand lightly.

"Jeez. You sure know how to make a girl feel good about herself." Secretly, I was feeling pretty damn good. I knew he didn't want, or need, complications in his life. But here I was.

"Bree—" he started.

"No. It's okay. I think I understand. You weren't looking for entanglements." I did pull my hand back now, pretending I needed something in my bag.

"It complicates the job." There was regret in his voice.

"I know. Do you know what your next assignment is going to be?" I dabbed the eye he couldn't see and wiped my nose with a tissue.

"You." A big smile formed on his face.

"Me?" I stopped rummaging in my bag and looked at him.

"Yeah. The mob is deep. Either Ledroit will run the family from prison, or one of her children will step up and take over. With or without her blessing. It's bound to be messy." He took my hand again.

"And you're afraid that they'll come after me?" I asked.

"It's fairly certain they will." Hambecker put his arm around my shoulder and pulled me to him but was stymied by the seat belt. He hit the release button so it retracted and he pulled me close. "Put the middle belt on," he said.

"Great. You get to be my babysitter." I wasn't sure how I felt about that. On one hand, I liked that he was going to be around, on the other—well let's just say I've never been good for babysitters. "I'm going to be a pain in the ass, you know."

"I'm counting on there being some perks to make up for it." He dropped a kiss on my head.

"Perks huh? I'll see what I can do." I liked the sound of perks.

"I'm counting on it. How's your leg?" He squeezed my shoulder.

"Hurting a little less." *Than a hot poker in the eye.*

"You're not just saying that so you can get laid, are you? What am I saying? Of course you're just saying that. You couldn't tell the truth to save your life."

"You are not calling me a liar." I was ready to do battle now. That was the trouble with Hambecker; he changed direction so quickly that it was hard to stay on my feet around him.

"No. I'm saying you are pathologically unable to tell the truth any time the truth interferes with what you want." He kissed me on the cheek.

"I'm getting kind of mad at you." I was trying to shrug his arm away, but it was impossible to get it to budge.

He grinned. "Good. Take your medicine and go back to sleep. I'm counting on that leg healing up really fast."

"You're impossible, you know that?" I smacked him on his thigh. Not very hard though. It didn't even sting my hand.

"Just keeping you on your toes. Take your meds." He nodded to my bag.

"I don't need them." *I really, really need them.*

"Don't make me treat you like a baby, Bree. If you don't take them in thirty minutes you're going to be hurting so bad you can't stand it. And it'll be thirty minutes after that before the meds start to work."

"Yeah, well I'm going to take them. But only

235

because I'm tired of listening to you talk. You're as bad as my older brother." I dragged the pills from my bag and swallowed them.

I was getting used to waking up in bed with Hambecker. It took me a minute to remember I was at Meg's house, and then the memory of my home, my dogs, caught up with me and my breath caught in my throat.

"Are you sick?" Hambecker was raspy with sleep.

"No. I'm okay. Reality just caught up with me." I wiped my eyes. "I'd forgotten."

He flexed his arm around me. "I'm sorry."

"Me too." I sniffed. "I can't get over the feeling I could have done something different. I could have saved them."

"Don't do that to yourself. Grieve. Cry. Wail. Curse the Gods. But don't make yourself responsible for what happened."

"Easy for you to say…" I started.

"Nope. We're done. Time to get up." He sat up, threw the covers off and pushed my legs off the bed. "Sad I can understand. This useless guilt irritates me. You want me to tape some plastic wrap over your dressing so you can shower?"

I sat on the edge of the bed, furious. What right did Richard Hambecker have to tell me how to feel? "Fuckity, fuck, fuck, fuck. What the hell, Hambecker?"

"Now there's a sentiment I can get behind. I'll be

back in a minute and you can swear at me some more."
He left the room.

"Well, shit." And then I started to laugh.

"What's so funny?" Hambecker asked when he came back in with plastic wrap and medical tape.

"You. One minute you're Mr. Sensitive the next you're a Drill Sergeant. I have no idea who you are at any given moment. It's funny as hell. Hey! Take it easy with the medical tape." I smacked his hand away. "Give me that."

"Go get in the shower. We've got stuff to do."

Chapter Sixteen

Hambecker, Meg and Tom were sitting at the kitchen table when I came down stairs. I rummaged in the cupboard for some Cheerios and a bowl and joined them. I spooned some cereal and milk into my mouth and asked, "So what's up?" when I noticed them all staring at me.

"Don't let my kids see you talking with your mouth full," Tom said. "Disgusting."

"Sorry," I said, my mouth full of cereal.

Hambecker laughed. I grinned at him. He was annoying, but I liked him anyway. I swallowed.

"I want to go back up to the farm today. Did Steve bring my truck here?" I asked.

"It's at the barracks, but Richard and I will go pick it up later. You weren't thinking of driving yourself up there were you?" Tom asked.

I shrugged.

"I'll take you up there," Meg said, "If you promise you'll write something today. I'm holding the front page for you."

"It's written. I just have to email it to you. It's big though, you might want to break it in two or something." I'd finished it before I'd left, in case I didn't come back.

"You might as well let me take her up," Hambecker broke in. "I'm not supposed to let her out of my sight."

"24/7?" Jeremy asked, walking in from the living room. "Man, that's rough." He grabbed some orange juice from the fridge and wandered back out again. I stuck my tongue out at his retreating back. *Teenagers.*

"That's fine for today, Bree," Tom said, "but at some point we need to discuss the ramifications of being on the mob's bad side."

"Do they have a good side?" I asked, raising my eyebrows.

"No. And that's the point. You're on their radar." Hambecker said. "Ledroit's trial won't come up for at least six months, that's a lot of time to stay vigilant."

"What do you think I should do?" I put more cereal in my mouth.

"Road trip," Meg said.

"But what about my job?" I asked.

"You can write on the road," she said.

"A little hard to write about what's happening in South Royalton when I'm not here, don't you think?" I put another spoonful of food in my mouth. I was really, really hungry today. I was feeling lighter than I had since the fire.

"You can do editorial pieces. Politics. Review the places you've been – we won't run them until you're long gone from them," Meg said.

"No." Hambecker said. "Too easy to extrapolate our route. No travel pieces."

"I could do travel pieces about places we don't go. Spain, say, and then Moscow," I said.

"We're off track again," Tom said. "You need a plan, and you need it soon. I'd say you have a day or two at most before they come after you."

"Can I go up to the farm first? I know you are all here at the table ready to make a plan, but I think better up there. And I want to check on Lucky."

Tom nodded and got up. "I've got to get to work anyway. Bring her to the barracks when she's done," he said to Hambecker.

"I'm coming with you," Meg said. "I want to be in on the planning session. I don't trust men not to miss an important detail."

The group around the table dispersed: Tom to work; Meg, Hambecker and I to Hambecker's SUV. The blackened shell of my home hadn't gotten any easier to look at, but I dashed the tears away and moved over to the grave. Someone had spray painted the rocks with gold metallic paint. It was like a pile of over-sized gold nuggets.

"Who did this?" Meg asked.

"I don't know, but I would assume Max or one of his grandkids. It's something he would do." I knelt down to pick up a rock that had slipped from the pile. "Can I have a minute?"

Me and Hambecker moved away and I put the stone back, leaving my hand resting on the warmth of the rock. I could feel my dogs around me, and Annabelle Cat too. Peace settled over me. Hambecker was right; they wouldn't want me to eat myself up with guilt. I'd done what I could about the person who murdered them. It was time to take care of myself.

"What do you think I should do about this?" I asked, as I joined Meg and Hambecker gazing at the house. "Rebuild, sell, leave it? What?"

"Tom thinks you should use some of the insurance money to buy one of those little RVs. You could travel around looking at different housing options so that when you come back you'll have an idea of what to build."

"Hambecker and I in an RV for six months. That ought to be interesting." Hell on wheels, I was guessing.

I went to sit on the pasture fence looking out over the valley. Lucky looked up from grazing and came to put his muzzle in my hand. I rubbed his head under his forelock, and pulled on his ears. He leaned his head into me, the way he always had. Footsteps rustled the grass behind me and Max came to stand beside me.

"I hear you'll be going off for a while," he said.

"Yeah, guess I have to." I rubbed the tips of Lucky's ears.

"Don't you be worrying about your boy here," he nodded his head in Lucky's direction, "I'll be taking good care of him."

"I know you will, Max. I'm sorry I won't be here to help with the horses."

"You remember when Mary was in the hospital with the cancer? You looked after the horses then, and more. All the animals up at t'house. I can take care of this one little pony for you." He laid a hand on my shoulder.

"Thanks, Max." I leaned my head on his hand.

"You just take care of yourself, you hear? Don't let those people be getting hold of you." He took a sugar cube from his pocket and let Lucky nuzzle it out of his hand.

"That's the plan," I said.

"Do you want me to have the house pulled down while you're away? We can get it ready for you to rebuild when you're ready." He leaned against the fence, looking over the valley.

"I'd like that Max."

"I'll get the Browns in to take it down. They'll have to do something special with those shingles, I suppose.

But they'll know what to do." He slapped his hand on the rail, like he'd made an important decision.

"Sounds good." I climbed off the fence and took a last look at the view. "I'll see you in a few months then." I hugged him.

"I had that skunk's stink gland removed. You want to take him with you?" he asked.

"Won't he be unhappy, cooped up in a motorhome all day?" The thought of Stripes made me smile.

"I doubt it. He's been spending the last couple of weeks sitting in Mary's lap while she watches TV. I asked if she wanted to keep him, but she can't get used to having a wild animal in the house. He'd be happy with you. I'll bring him down to Meg's for you, when I come to say goodbye." He said.

I nodded my throat tight from the thought of saying goodbye to Max.

"Now don't you be crying. It's not forever. In another year it will all be back to normal." He hugged me and turned away, making his way back up the hill to his home.

I hoped he was right. I had a feeling that trials involving the mob didn't always go smoothly. Some poor soul would probably shoot me coming out of the courthouse because Ledroit had promised to take care of his family if he killed me. If they didn't get to me before then. I wondered how the trial would go without my testimony. They had Victor; he was more important than I was.

I spent a minute more soaking in the sunshine and the smell of long grass and horses. This had always been my favorite place in the world, now I was going to go looking for other places. Something to replace the house that I had loved.

I sighed, and joined Meg and Hambecker at the SUV. "I'm ready."

I took one last look around before I got in the car. I would never feel the same about this place again. That made me sad. But it made it a hell of a lot easier to leave.

The plan, when it came together, was simple. A small RV with my motorcycle strapped to a trailer on the back. No phone. Except for Hambecker who had one so that his boss could contact him. I could email Tom who would cut and paste my messages to my family, and then send them along, but no phone calls not even from payphones. Not that there were many of those left around. Beans and Stripes would go with us, although Tom thought long and hard about vetoing Stripes. Tom thought Stripes would make us too memorable, but I promised to keep him out of sight.

I went online in the incident room, clicking around, looking for an RV I might actually like the look of. There were some really cool, space age looking RVs, and some funky, gypsy caravan-like contraptions built into pickup trucks but Hambecker vetoed them.

"Need to blend in. Think bland, ordinary," he said, then he went back to talking to Tom.

"Bland *schmand*," I muttered under my breath, and switched my focus to vehicles that were plain on the outside but unique on the inside. I was not living in an ugly motor home. Meg came to sit beside me.

"They're ugly," I said. "Truly ugly."

"Just get a generic one and I'll help you decorate the inside. You could pick up little things to add in each of the places you stop," she said.

"Uh-huh. That'd be me. Driving around the country in a vehicle stuffed full of knickknacks and one really cranky Federal Agent." I snorted.

"You don't sound too happy about this."

"Would you be?" I asked.

"No. But I've got the kids to take care of." She bit her lips as if she thought she'd said the wrong thing.

"It just doesn't seem like me, driving around like a snail with my house on my back. We should be taking the train across America, or riding bikes." I could picture myself on a motorcycle pulling a little trailer, just big enough to sleep in. But where would the animals sit? Especially in bad weather.

"Motorcycles or bicycles?" Meg asked.

"Both. Either. Doesn't matter. A convertible, pulling a little tear-drop trailer. Not a motor-home. That's for old people," I said.

"You're going to have trouble with the blending-in thing aren't you?" She looked at me with something akin to pity.

"What do you think?" I asked, and then sighed. "I'll do what it takes.

"Come on, Hambecker is driving us home," Meg said.

"Call him The Hammer. He likes that." I laughed.

"Really, you aren't pulling my leg?" she asked.

"No, he likes it." I kept a straight face.

When Meg called into Tom's office "Hey Hammer Man, we're ready to go home."

Hambecker gave me a dirty look and said, "I'll deal

with you later."

I experienced an obscene amount of glee from the exchange and sang in the car on the way home. He glared at me, but didn't tell me to stop. I sang louder. Traveling with Hambecker had its possibilities.

The next morning, Meg and I were at the paper. Deirdre was putting the finishing touches on the front page, complete with a photo of me with raccoon eyes. We were going live with the online version of the story at midnight. The physical copy would be on the stands in the morning. The exclusive coverage of the murder and mayhem that would follow was going a long way to reassure our advertisers. Even the Valley News was going to have to wait to run the piece.

Lucy Howe waltzed in just as I was packing up to leave. "Bree, just the person I was hoping to see. Can I get an interview?" She smiled her sweetest, ass-kissing smile and I knew it was killing her to have to ask.

"What for?" I asked. I could see Meg laughing silently behind her computer.

"I'm working for the Valley News now," Lucy said.

"Didn't they tell you? They bought the piece direct from me. The Valley News already has it." I looked at her as innocently as I could.

Lucy's face turned bright red. She opened her mouth and closed it. "Well, fuck me," she said, and turned on her heel and left. Her footsteps banged down the stairs.

"Someone's in for an ass chewing," Meg said. "I wouldn't want to be the one in charge when she hits the newsroom."

"I'd sure like to be a fly on the wall, though," I said. "I bet you she goes ballistic."

Heavy footsteps sounded on the stairs and Tom came in and walked to Meg's desk. "How's it going, babe? Got the paper handled?" He dropped a kiss on her mouth and came over to sit at my desk. "Come on you two, we've got something to show you."

Meg and I followed Tom downstairs. Parked against the green was the plainest brown, tan and almost white RV I'd ever seen. It wasn't ugly so much as totally without personality. I sighed.

"That's it?" I asked.

"Come see the inside." Tom grabbed Meg's and my hand and towed us across the street. Hambecker appeared at the door, hopped down and slid out the steps.

"You're kidding me," I said. "You couldn't find anything a little less bland than this?"

"Go inside and look." Hambecker grinned at me.

I pulled myself up the steps and into another world. The interior was old world gypsy. The ceiling was rounded and paneled in golden pine. The woodwork and cabinets painted in bright reds, greens and gold designs. A heavy regal curtain hung below a carved bulkhead separating the living area from the bedroom. A gold fabric valance graced the window above the sink.

"It's a gypsy caravan!" I laughed. "I'm a gypsy."

I spotted the richly-upholstered couch and a hoot of pure joy escaped me. On the center cushion, curled around each other and sound asleep, were Beans and

Stripes. The backs of my eyeballs got all tingly and I blinked hard.

"No waterworks, now." Hammie pulled me close and wrapped his arms around me. "Or I'll have to do something stupid so you'll want to kick my ass."

I wrapped my arms around Hammie's bulk. "I always feel like kicking your ass." I stretched up to kiss him.

"I'm out of here," Meg said.

"Right behind you." Tom slammed the door as he jumped down.

Beans woke up and started barking, and I broke the kiss to shush him. Stripes was looking up at me sleepily, and I felt a surge of gratitude toward Max for having him de-skunked. I pulled free of Hammie to pick him up.

"Fuck." He ran his hand across his close cropped head. "I'm going to come second to a skunk and his tiny ass dog, aren't I?"

I grinned up at Hammie, stroking Stripes' soft black and white coat. "Yep," I said. "Pretty much."

Afterward

The early morning mist was rising off the deserted stretch of river where Hambecker and I had parked the day before. The leaves hanging over the water had begun to turn, and were reflected on the surface under the drifting mist. I bent over and cupped the clear water and splashed it on my face. Not too bad. I dropped my towel on the ground, stripped off my sweats and T-shirt, and stood naked on the shore.

I stepped into the slow moving water and shivered. There was only one way to do this without torturing myself; I dove into the deeper water and came up in the faster water midstream gasping.

"Cold!" I struck out for the opposite shore, swimming hard to warm my body, feeling the chill tighten my skin. I steadied myself with my hand on a boulder once there, breathing hard. I pushed off and swam back, the water like silk between my legs.

Hambecker was on the shore with Beans and Stripes when I stepped out of the water. "Here," he said, and folded me into my towel. I turned to kiss him, letting the towel fall to slip my arms around his neck. I teased his lips with my tongue and he deepened the pressure sliding his tongue into my mouth. My brain had gone south, I tightened my hold around his neck and wrapped my legs around his hips.

Hambecker groaned deep in his throat and slid his hands under my thighs rubbing his erection against me until I threw back my head.

"Dear God, Hambecker," I could barely get the words out.

His licked the hollow above my collarbone and blew his hot breath on the damp depression before pressing a kiss there. My nipples contracted so tightly they ached.

"Take me inside," I whispered, and then laughed nervously at the double meaning.

"Are you laughing at me?" Hambecker bit my shoulder lightly. "You shouldn't do that."

I pulled myself tight against him, rubbed my body against him and grinned as he groaned.

"What's the matter Hammer Man? Can't take a joke?" I sucked in my breath as he brushed his fingers between my thighs. "Oh God. Please. Take me to bed."

He turned then and carried me to the ugly-on-the-outside RV. He whistled for Beans and Stripes. Beans ran up the steps like lightning, but we had to wait for Stripes to waddle along and pull himself up the steps. I bounced with impatience until Hambecker followed him in and pulled the door shut.

He carried me to the back and set me on our bed, pulling closed the heavy curtains to keep the animals in the dinette.

"I didn't realize how handy those curtains were going to be," He said as he pulled his shirt over his head. He shucked his jeans, his erection springing up as the material slid down his legs.

"Hurry." I was fire and ice, needing him inside me.

He pulled a condom from the drawer beside the bed, but he didn't open the package. Instead he traced the scar on my thigh. He bent and kissed it, sending shivers through me.

"Please."

He pushed my legs apart and kissed my inner thighs. He slid two fingers into me, finding my G-spot as he took my clit with his tongue. My hips raised to meet his lips as the tension rose and broke inside me, leaving me dizzy.

"That must have been some kind of speed record," Hambecker said moving up to lay beside me.

I laughed a little breathlessly. "You're not getting off that easy. Oh God, that's so dirty." I snorted.

I pushed him over onto his back and tore open the condom, rolling it down over his erection. Then I straddled him, teasing for a moment, before lowering myself so he slid into me. I tried to keep my mind, riding him hard and deep until he came. But in the end it was all mindless passion as he raked his teeth across my nipples and we came in a rush of physical sensation.

We lay nestled together dozing until I felt him growing large between my legs.

"Wanna go again?" I asked.

He groaned and pulled me close. "On one condition," he said.

"What condition?" I snuggled back rubbing my butt against him to feel him harden even more.

"We go at my speed," he whispered in my ear.

"What speed is that?" I asked.

"I'll show you." He rolled me over and pinned me on my back, taking my earlobe between his teeth and nipping gently. Then his tongue slid along my jaw line followed by his warm breath. The sensation of warmth against my cool, moist skin gave me shivers, and my nipples hardened. A fire was building low in my belly, insisting we move things along. But Hambecker wouldn't be hurried.

He dragged his tongue across the tips of my nipples and when I started to buck my hips, he held me down with his arm across my thighs so all I could do was writhe with need.

"Hambecker," I pleaded. "Richard…"

"Using my given name? That's new. What's the matter Bree?" But he didn't wait for an answer. He licked into my belly button, kissing my stomach and making his way down my thigh. Achingly slow he kissed the bottoms of my feet, stopping to massage the fleshy pads above my toes with his fingers.

I was quivering with tension by the time he made his way up the inside of my thigh with little kisses, my body one gigantic nerve under his touch. Hambecker spread my legs further with his knees and hesitated to slide on a condom. I closed my eyes and felt him pulse slowly into me moving deeper and deeper into me with infinitesimal movements, his strokes so slow that my nerve endings were screaming for release when he finally pushed the whole of his erection inside of me, and waited there.

I quivered there, suspended, wanting to buck, to rub my swollen clit against the root of his penis. But the weight of his hips held me down, punishing me with stillness.

"Richard…"

He pulled out of me again, millimeter by millimeter, the slowest retreat in the history of mankind. My brain was flooded with sensation, my hands fisted in the bed clothes.

"Richard…"

He broke the tension. Sliding in and out of me with power and speed until I crashed around him, shattered, and he joined me.

We lay together for quite a while, just breathing. My mind eventually came back to me and I kissed his neck, damp with sweat and tasting of salt.

"Wow." What more was there for me to say?

Hambecker raised himself up on to his elbows and grinned down at me. "Did I do okay?" he asked with mock humility.

I smacked him on the shoulder and he rolled me over on top of him sliding out of me. I kissed him again, on the lips this time.

"I'm hungry," I said, batting my eyes at him.

"Grill cheese sandwich and tomato soup?"

"Perfect," I said. And it really was.

The End

**If you enjoyed this book, other Bree
MacGowan mysteries are available now!**

Moonlighting In Vermont
California Schemin'

Meet Author Kate George

Ms. George has enjoyed a life-long love affair with mysteries, and by age 25 had written her first book, a truly awful novella. She then wisely took a break from writing. When Ms. George realized that she could use her own off-beat sense of humor in her work, she began writing seriously again. Ms. George loves animals, and they find their way into her writing. The incident with the crazy skunk in *California Schemin'* (March 2011) is a true account. For the record, the dogs would rather stink than be washed with peroxide, baking soda or dishwashing soap ever again.